SHAIDA was raised as a child in Kashmir, Pakistan. She spent the majority of her life in London, England. She was educated in London and later received a BA Honours degree after taking time out to raise a family.

Her experiences of past life are shared with the society of today.

'So far ahead in the world we have come,
And yet, deep down inside,
We are still so far away.'

TEARS BEHIND THE VEIL

A True Story

TEARS BEHIND THE VEIL

A True Story

SHAIDA MEHRBAN

ATHENA PRESS LONDON

ISBN 978 1 84748 315 7

First published 2008 by
ATHENA PRESS
Queen's House, 2 Holly Road
Twickenham TW1 4EG
United Kingdom

*This is a true story. The names of the
characters in this book have been changed.*

Printed for Athena Press

To the memory of my father, who passed away over ten years ago, and who I loved very much but somehow respected a whole lot more. He played the role of the father and mother with dignity, as my mother died over forty years ago. That delicate relationship between a father and daughter was emotionally woven with strict guidelines. No matter how close a daughter needed to be to her father, he kept that gap for a safe haven, while she bridged it with respect. He was a proud father and always believed in his children, irrespective of whether they were male or female.

This is the second in a series of true stories taken from around the world. The stories explore the lives of ordinary women within the male-dominated household, their struggles and the reality of their hardship. They share their thoughts on how they feel when coming to terms with specific compromises within their religion and culture. A struggle results when they share their frustration about their lifestyle, which demands empathy with and respect for the man because he is the dominant head of the household and keeper of the wife. At times, the only way he gains total control is through force, whether through dominance or domestic, sexual, physical or verbal violence. Is it any wonder even today, women feel like 'second-class citizens'?

Education, television, radio and the media have meant that women are now opening up their minds to the difference between their reality and the actual lifestyle of other women around the world. They're forced to face the unaddressed subject of oppression and inequality and the effects of these factors on them as mothers, sisters, daughters and wives.

Their own struggles have opened their eyes and minds to the fact that they want something better for their female offspring. How can their thoughts bring about change in a society that has become used to the man leading and the female following, a life where women can be seen but not heard, especially if they're speaking for equality?

The first story, *Tears of Silence*, began in Kashmir, Pakistan. This second story raises issues of great sensitivity. It is 2008 and yet things are still not as equal as they should be. Will they ever be? Will it be like this for ever? But then, who knows what for ever is?

This story is set in the beautiful, scenic Esholt in the Yorkshire dales. The beauty of nature and the human's survival of nurture are both captivated in this story of Sania Hema Craven, a young girl with an English father and an Indian mother. Sania – a girl culturally enriched by both parents. The story really begins with the death of a member of her family and goes from bad to worse as she is taken back to her parent's roots where her life is just a mere existence. Finally, after years of disarray, she makes some painful choices. Sania makes these decisions in this story but, in real life, Hema, who did live in this beautiful place, made all these choices and did go to her mother's birthplace. This is why the name of the location in India has been omitted.

Many thanks must go to Hema, who trusted me to use my words to describe her pain. I would also like to thank Parveen, who was the real name behind the first book's character, Kaashi, and who felt that I had done justice to the story of her painful life.

Contents

Killer Child

I WAS A happy child. I had a perfect life. There was my mum, my dad and me, Sania Hema Craven, an English girl born and bred in the heart of the beautiful scenery of the Yorkshire Dales. My parents were my pride and joy. My father, Doctor Thomas Craven, was a reputable citizen of the community serving the sick and needy. Radika, my mother, had been our strength, nurturing us both, supporting and taking care of us and meeting all our needs. He was the provider; she was the carer, full-time.

My life would not have been complete without either of them. I always feared losing my mother. As a child I never wanted to have a life without her, but my father was my lifeline. I never feared for my father for he was our knight in shining armour; he protected us. Every time I saw him coming home, parking his car, putting the key in the door, I would be standing in the hallway with the biggest smile and a twinkle in my eye. He, as always, would put his bag down, pick me up and fuss over me. I was the centre of his life, or rather he was mine.

It was a day like any other day – a typical Monday, the first Monday of October – and I had come home from school, walking with my friends as usual. As I reached my house I could see my mother waiting for me with the door wide open. She smiled at me, and carried on looking until I kissed her on the cheek.

'Hi, Mama.'

'Hello, Sania. Did you have a good day?'

'Yes, Mama. Listen, I was chosen as the captain for the hockey team again this year.'

'Oh, for heaven's sake, Sania, is there a day that you don't talk about sports or boys? Please let me hear something about your study or girls instead. Please, child, just for one day.'

'Mama, I'm only in year eight. I'll study later. Let me have some fun for now.'

As I took off my school uniform, the smell of food being cooked aroused my taste buds. I quickly put on my joggers and a top, and ran downstairs to eat.

'Sania, how many times have I told you to wear our own clothes – or if not, at least trousers, and not joggers and T-shirts all the time like a boy.'

'Oh, Mama!'

'Don't Mama me. You're thirteen years old and still, as always, even on this birthday, you went shopping again with your father and brought joggers and T-shirts.'

'Mama, I promise, on my next birthday I'll buy some trousers, but until then joggers it is.'

There was a knock at the door and I hurriedly went to open it, quickly slipping my trainers on. At this time of the day the boys in the neighbourhood always played football outside, and today was no exception.

As I stood in goal I could see my father's Mercedes drive up the road. I ran to him.

'Goal, goal, yeah,' one of the boys shouted.

'Sani, because of you we lost, you idiot,' another boy shouted after me.

My day felt worthwhile as my father kissed my forehead. He cuddled me and walked me to the house.

'Sani,' he said, 'don't tell your mother, but I've brought your football boots for you today.'

'OK, Papa. Mama's already had a go about the joggers; why upset her more!'

We both looked at each other, smiling.

'Hello, Radi,' my father said to his wife.

'What's this "hello"?' my mother said in reply. 'Why can't you speak in our own language, like other normal people, Tom? Father and daughter are exactly the same, both always in English clothes and with English tongues. Honestly, I don't know when this girl is ever going to learn…'

'Have you been giving your mother a hard time today?' interrupted Papa.

'No, Papa, really, I was my normal self.'

'No wonder. But child, why can't you wear your own Asian clothes when you come home if it makes her happy? Just for one day!'

Laughing, I replied, 'Papa, football boots and a sari?'

We both laughed aloud and were in fits of giggles when Mama came in with food for us.

'Yes laugh, carry on. Why don't we have English food every day? After all, you both look and behave like true Westerners, so why do you eat *desi*, Asian food? Make my life easier, too. Fish and chips from the chippy every day on your way back from school.'

Mama always spoke to Papa as if he was an Indian – just like her.

'Oh, Mama.'

'I told you, don't Mama me.'

As Papa moved from the sofa to the dining table, I moved with him. All was quiet. I was about to open my mouth again, when suddenly he put his finger on his lips to quieten me. I looked at him as he smiled at my mama.

I smiled, he smiled back.

He nodded, my smile got wider.

We both sat quietly while Mama served food for us all. We sat silently through the first course. Mama and Papa both slowly glanced at one another but exchanged no words. We moved onto our main course and then Papa broke the silence by saying how good the food was. Mama knew he was just trying to make small talk. She rolled her eyes at him.

Suddenly her facial expression changed and she became calm once more. 'Honestly, can't you find something better to talk about than food? Anyway, listen, your brother phoned from London just to remind you to send him the things he ordered as soon as you can.'

'Yes, I know,' said Papa, 'I have already spoken to someone about getting the things out to him...'

By the time we finished our meal everyone was laughing and we were at peace with one another again. Papa and I moved over to the sofa to watch the television, while Mama cleared the table.

The laughter on the box became dimmer and my eyes stopped fluttering as much. The fullness of the day weighed on them almost to the point of not being able to keep them open any more. I could feel the sweat from my forehead running down my cheeks because of Papa's body heat next to mine. I smiled, knowing that he was sitting while I was sleeping on his shoulder, no care in the world. I felt safe.

'Sania, move. Sania, move! For God's sake, move!'

'Shhh... let me sleep.'

I opened my eyes. The more Mama tried to pull me away from Papa, the stronger my grip became around his neck.

'Mama, please, let me sleep on Papa's shoulder,' I cried loudly. 'Anyway, Papa's also asleep. Please, Mama.'

She took one look at me and then, with all her might, she pulled me to the floor.

'Mama, mama...'

'Just shut up, I mean it!' Her face was furious, as I had never seen it before. Her eyes were so wide that they scared me.

I sat looking at her, silently now. All I could hear was, 'Breathe, please breathe, for Sania's sake. Please breathe, Tom.'

She kept touching his face and chest, but what for?

The doorbell rang and I quickly got up from the floor and opened the door.

'Hello, is Mrs Craven in?'

'Come in. Hurry, please. In here,' she replied.

The ambulance was waiting outside with its light flashing. As I watched the two men walk calmly past me, I tried really hard to put the pieces of the puzzle together.

'Mama, what's happening?'

'Nothing, dear, go to your room.'

'Mama, what are these men doing to Papa?'

'I told you, just go to your room. Now!'

'Papa, you tell me, what's happening? Please, Papa.'

'Stay away. He's fine.'

'Papa, what are they doing to you? Please, Papa.'

'Didn't I tell you to go to your room? He is fine,' insisted Mama. 'Now go! Please child, I beg you. For your father's sake, go up.'

For my father's sake, I would do anything. I moved myself through the hallway and started to climb the stairs. I knew that if I went halfway up, just around the bend of the stairs, I would be out of her sight but still see what was happening. I sat with my arms folded around my knees and my head resting on them. My tears were running without hesitation. I cried but made no more noise as I did not want to upset anyone. I sniffed quietly to stop my runny nose, but the emotional turmoil inside me was much too great for me to bear. I wanted to cry out loud and be heard, but I knew that I ought to listen this time.

The ambulance men went out and then, quickly this time and not calmly, came back in with something big in their hands. Then, in an instant, that object became a bed and someone was lying on it. That someone was covered with a pure colour: a white, lifeless cloth. What did that mean? Was I expecting the worst? How did I know that was a bed that someone was lying on? I knew because I had seen a stretcher before at a football match that Papa and I went to see. One of the players got hurt and instantly the stretcher came, and he was gone. Who was gone now?

The white cloth I knew covered someone as there were humps and bumps underneath. At a family funeral I had seen a body covered in a pure, clinical cloth like this one.

That's how I knew that whoever was lying in the shadow of the cloth was no longer in our lives. I knew who it was, even though I did not want to admit it.

I was so engrossed in my thoughts that I did not hear anyone coming up the stairs. My mother was standing on the corner step looking at me. We both fixed our eyes on one another; no words, just tears. My eyes were full of questions, her tears were full of all the answers. I opened my mouth to ask my biggest question.

'Mama—'

'No, child,' Mama broke in. 'Now listen carefully.'

'No, Mama, don't do this. Please tell me—'

'Now listen, child, you are my good child who listens to her mama, don't you? Yes, of course you are.'

As she clasped my face in her hands, she continued, 'I am going out. It's late now, child, so you go up and go to sleep. Charlie is already here and she will stay with you until I get back. If you need her she'll be in the lounge. Now please, child, go to sleep.'

Charlie was our faithful neighbour and dear friend. But I didn't need her; I needed Mama!

'Mama, please—'

'No, child, sleep now.'

'No!'

'Yes.'

'Not until you tell me where Papa is.'

'I've told you, don't worry, he'll be fine.'

'Where is he then? Is he…?'

'No, quiet. He's, uh… he'll be fine.

'Where is he?'

'Uh, uh… he's here, of course.'

'Is he? I want to see him!'

'You will, just not now. He's going out with me; in fact he has already left. Now I have to go, child.'

'Was that him on the—'

'Have faith, child, in the good Lord. Pray he will look after all of us, and I mean *all*.'

'Mama…'

'No more, silence. Now go. And remember, child, no more tears please.'

'And you, Mama, your tears?'

I got up to hug her. She looked at me coldly as she held my arms and put a distance between us. She was a broken woman, as it was only in extreme circumstances that she would create such distance between us. I remembered the last time when… when… yes, I know, when her father died. It was the same feeling: cold, heartless, deliberate, shutting the doors on me, on my face, on my tears, on her only child. She knows what it's like: she is an only child as well.

She wanted to be ignorant of my feelings but it was impossible for me. I moved my arm from her grasp as I wiped her tears with my hand. For a split second I saw the warmth of her motherly love shine through her eyes as they gazed at me, but then, in the next instant, she turned away and went down. Charlie stood at the bottom of the steps now, as my mama pushed past her.

'Hey Sani, you OK?'

With tears running down my face, I replied unconvincingly, 'Yes, of course.'

I lay awake in my bed, hugging the only comfort I had, my soft and cuddly four-foot-long monkey called Cookie. He stared at my neck as I held him close. I stared at the ceiling for so long that my head was swirling.

'Cookie, he will be all right, won't he?'

I lifted his face so he was now looking at me – no reply. His face, as always, was sad, lifeless, ugly and dark – all the things I hated, but I still loved him. He never disappointed me or disciplined me, just listened and kept all my secrets. He was my favourite cuddly toy from childhood. As my sobbing silenced, I could feel that my eyes were heavy and puffy. However hard I tried to stop them, tears rolled down my cheeks and fell into the pools of my ears. All of a sudden I could hear recognisable footsteps. They were coming up the stairs. My senses reawakened once again. I quickly sat up and dried the tears from my ears. The door opened quietly and there she stood, her eyes red, her nose sore and her face pale. I sat silently, cuddling Cookie.

'Oh God, Sania, how many times have I told you not to go to sleep with your joggers on? And today you have disobeyed me ever further by wearing your trainers in bed as well. Tut-tut, shame on you, Sania.'

I quickly raced to the door, to run down the stairs. She grabbed me as I tried to get past.

'You're hurting me, Mama.'

'Hurting? You haven't experienced hurting yet, but now you will.'

'Mama, you're hurting me, let go!'

Her grip on my wrist tightened as she blurted out in a fury, 'You've hurt me for the first and last time, you bitch.'

'Bitch? Me, Mama? Why, Mama, why?'

'You'll never be forgiven, child, you… you…'

'What, Mama? Let me go, let me go to Papa.'

'You have killed him, you evil bitch. Yes, you, innocent little Sania – *killer child*, bad girl, never did what you were told. Happy now?'

'Who have I killed, Mama?'

'Don't Mama me, you know very well; your dear Papa, my love, my only love.'

My life, my dad; my life, my dad – no more because of me? Yes, I am what my mama said, a 'killer child'. Yes, I killed my father. I am a bad girl; Sani very bad girl, killed her dad, I am bad, I killed my dad, I am a killer. Cookie, I am a bad girl, I killed my father, I am a killer…

I wept silently in the corner of the room, sitting on the floor with Cookie on my lap. I felt all alone as I wept tears of loneliness. No one was there to comfort me and there was no one who wanted to be comforted by me, especially not her.

Tears of loneliness wept by the killer child. Yes, that was me.

I did not even know what time it was, but I knew that it was very early morning as the light was beaming through my curtains. It was no longer dark outside, but in here it was very dark. I must have dozed off quickly as I was unaware of my own existence any more.

Deathly Reunion

THAT MORNING I woke up not knowing what to expect or to think, especially because I had only slept a couple of hours – my head was not clear at all. I went downstairs to see my mother doing her normal chores: cleaning and tidying up, trying very hard to deliberately avoid any eye contact with me.

Charlie was on the phone to someone, looking sombre.

'Did you sleep well, Sani?' she asked slowly.

'Not really, Charlie, I didn't even realise that I had dozed off.'

'What do you mean?'

'After Mother left my room I sat in the corner on the rug and cried myself to sleep. The sunshine through the window woke me up. Just as well as my bum's a bit sore.'

'Stop talking rubbish and quickly have breakfast,' interjected Mother. 'We need to go out for a while. Charlie, stop encouraging her.'

'Where are we going, Mama?'

'Stop asking and just do what you're told for once in your life!'

As I sat still taking in Mother's harsh words, Charlie signalled for me to keep quiet and do what I was told. I quickly made myself a cup of tea and went upstairs. As I scrambled around to find my trainers and joggers from yesterday I realised that I still had them on. I had dozed off with them still on. As I was about to leave the room after tidying myself up, I thought that today I should really not upset Mother, so I closed the door again and took the joggers and trainers off.

I changed into my sari and sandals and, like a lady, I neatly brushed my hair the way Mother always taught me to. As I looked in the mirror I could have mistaken the person looking at me for my mother. As I entered the kitchen, Charlie looked at me, smiling.

'Oh my Lord, Sani, your beautiful long hair, it's so long! You are looking so ladylike today. I really didn't know that underneath the cap and joggers there lived a lady.'

As Charlie was speaking, my mother looked from the corner of her eye; I knew she approved. Otherwise she would have looked at me and given that disappointed look.

'Shall we go?' she said quietly.

'Yes,' I replied. I dared not ask her where today. She instantly went to the front door. She didn't open it. Instead she looked down at me, no feeling, nothing, except a pale, blank look. She put her hand onto my father's car keys. Her own were hanging next to his.

I quickly blurted out, 'They're Papa's.' She looked at me, then very quietly told me that everything of my papa's was now hers. As I looked into her empty eyes I remembered how I always used to say to her when in a hurry, 'Oh, just use Papa's keys,' and she always refused. However, today the attitude had changed, although she still looked the same woman – slender, tall and as always well presented. Her long hair had beautifully covered her small waist, which she always paraded in her sari. Today was no exception.

Our journey was cold and silent; throughout I just watched her hands on the wheel and the gear stick. Fifteen minutes into the journey I started to recollect my memory of this fearful, knowing journey. My hands turned into fists of sweat, my forehead was damp with frustration and panic. I didn't want this to be true but it was. Yes it was. How I wished that it wasn't. I kept looking at her. She never looked at me, not even once, but in this same seat Father had looked so many times, smiling as always. But now a new owner, a new role, same position.

Oh Lord, I wish it wasn't.

'Get out of the car.'

I ignored her, and now I was not looking at her. Suddenly, the car door was open. She removed my seat belt. I held tightly onto the sides of my seat. She pulled me. I grabbed the seat tighter. I kept saying 'no, no', without looking at her, but suddenly I felt a tear drop onto my sari. I looked at her; her eyes were wet. I let go of the car seat and got out quietly. I held her swinging hand; she brushed it away. She in front, me behind. I dared not look around as someone might recognise me, and not because of my clothes. 'Wait here for me.' I did what she asked.

'Follow me,' was all she said, and our journey resumed. We entered a building, and then went through another door. She talked to someone and then said that we were both ready. I started to think really hard. Ready for what?

All of a sudden the room felt cold. As I looked around I saw a trolley, and an eerie feeling ran down my spine; my heart started to beat fast, almost as if it was going to explode. The white, pure colour of death was in front of me, the only difference was that the stretcher was now a cold, silver trolley on wheels. I moved back to the door and stood almost glued to it. As I looked away from death, I looked at my mother who, for the first time since yesterday, was looking straight into my eyes, sharp and calculating.

'Come closer, Sania,' she said.

'No, Mama.'

'I said, come closer, come closer to me, now!'

I felt frightened and, above all, intimidated, as she came over to me and grabbed my hand really hard. She told a man who was in the room with us to leave, as she wanted to be alone. I didn't want to make a scene but I could not contain my tears any more. I cried out screams of a small animal rather than that of an adolescent. She asked me to look at the person lying on the trolley. I refused. She insisted. I turned my face away until I could hide no more. She grabbed me by the hair and pushed my face right on top of it. She pulled back the sheet. It was my papa. My beloved papa – silent, fast asleep, peaceful. I sighed.

'You couldn't get enough of your father. Now, enjoy your *deathly reunion* with him – it will be your last.'

My nose was so close to him that I could smell him. But today he didn't smell of his scent; instead it was of medicine. He didn't look back as I kept saying, 'Papa, open your eyes, for my sake, please, please.'

This pleading was all to no avail. Suddenly, Mother let go of my hair. I started to kiss his face and hand. She watched. I could hear bells ringing in my ears and hurricane winds blowing my hair. 'Oh no, help!'

'Papa.' I opened my eyes and looked around. My mother was standing by me. She asked me if I was all right now. I nodded. She told me to get up slowly as I may faint again if I got up quickly. I told her that I needed to see Father again. She told me, simply, that my reunion with my father was over; this was my personal time with him, but no more.

She held my hand and escorted me out and then into the car. I was distraught and confused and for a moment wished that I was no longer alive, but then she saved me and made me feel good again by holding my hand.

'Mama—'

'Shhh.'

We both sat in the empty house all alone; the doorbell rang a few times but neither of us opened the door. I looked at her many times; she always ignored my glance. She was silent. I was confused. We both lay on the sofa together in silence, thinking. I felt lonely but her world had been torn apart. And why? Yes, because of 'killer child'. That's why she kept her distance from me. Silence, loneliness and tears.

The clock struck six. I looked at the front door. No one came in; I was not playing outside and there was still silence inside. This was the time that Papa was supposed to come home. *O Lord, please make it happen*, I thought. *I'll be a really good girl and do everything asked of me. Just bring Papa back.*

Suddenly the door opened. I got up, startled.

'Papa?'

'Sani, it's me.'

'Oh, Charlie, I thought...'

'You thought what?'

'Nothing.'

She went on to explain that she came to bring us both some food as she knew we would not be up to making any ourselves. My mother just left the room and went upstairs. After a few minutes her door slammed shut. I told Charlie I did not want to eat. She left it, so that maybe I could eat it later. As she sat down she put my head in her lap and told me that everything would be all right. 'It will take time and time is a good healer.'

I told her that I was the reason that Father died, that Mother had told me so and had labelled me the 'killer child'. That's why she was keeping her distance from me. In reply, Charlie tried to reassure me that none of that was true and that Mother was just trying to cope in the best way she could by blaming someone. That someone just happened to be me and, at the moment, I was the closest person to her.

A week had gone by but things had not got any better. The day of the funeral arrived and the house was full of strangers – my father's family. My mother's family did not attend.

They were not on speaking terms with her since she married a white man, going against her religion and against her parents' wishes. Father came from a small family. Charlie pointed out my grandparents as I recollected my minimal memories of them. Our neighbours all gathered around to support us in our difficult time.

For a whole week I had been wearing a sari; it was almost as if the white cloth from my father had been draped around me for a week. We both wore white, a widow and an orphan. The priest recited holy rituals for the day of the funeral and I still remember how I looked on to get a glimpse of my father's face for the last time. It was an impossible task as my grandparents stayed beside the coffin the whole time. Now his presence was seen only in his photograph, for ever.

The graveyard that my friends and I had often ridden our bikes through to cut our long journey down almost looked like a scene from a horror movie today. I felt scared going in and yet I hadn't before. Today my journey served the real purpose of the graveyard – his burial.

My father no more, just memories.

They say that school teaches and prepares you for life, but no school, not even my private independent school, could have prepared me for this. The cemetery where my father was buried never saw the happy girl playing in its vicinity ever again. Now it only saw a scared child going in to ask the Lord to give her father back to her. Many times I would plead for my father to come back: *O Lord put him together again, put the bones back together into a skeleton again, put new flesh on the bones and create life for me.*

The next few weeks were sombre: neighbours, family and friends would come in the morning and join us for another long day sitting on the floor. We all wore white – a sign of respect, cleanliness and a mood of thoughtful serenity. We sat on the white, clean cloth and faced the priest, who recited his holy rituals and shared many wise words with his audience, who for weeks was us.

Mother made sure that she reminded me that we both couldn't brush our hair during this period. She knew that after a few days I was dying to take the knots out. As I started to open my long plait she would look at me sternly and, shaking her head, would say, 'No.' For a split second we both almost looked identical, except for the difference in years, as we sat and looked into each other's eyes.

'Mama,' I began.

'Shush now, child, not now.'

'But when, Mama?'

'I said, didn't I, shush.'

The only reaction she saw now were the tears running down my cheeks. She didn't want to acknowledge them, so she looked away.

In a way I was distraught to have had this week. But looking back on it now, maybe that time was well spent. I thought about my future life – a life where I would spend hours looking at my father's photograph, him staring back at me, no smile, just silent. That was the only form of my father I had left to live with. She, alive and silent, through choice; he dead and silent, without choice. And me, sad, silent and depressed.

Fresh Memories, Uncertain Future

IT WAS THE beginning of December now, a couple of months had gone by and things at home were becoming stable to some extent, nearer to normal at least. That is, a normal that I had never witnessed before.

One thing that was good, for sure, was that the majority of people coming had stopped. The white, serene covering of the floor with all white, live bodies had also decreased. Neighbours and friends were also coming less, which gave us the strength and quietness to think, and more so, reflect on this sombre and bleak period.

Christmas had come and gone unnoticed, and so had New Year's Day, while the big picture at the front of the room on the floor remained for these three months. As did the daily aroma of the deadly, especially at this time, over-exaggerated, smelly fumes of the incense sticks which had to be lit first thing in the morning. When we awoke we would go to the bathroom and then carry out our very first daily duty to the good Lord for giving us this new day and show our gratitude to the one who has blessed us. Before we, all three of us, gathered around the small prayer room, lit the incense stick, offered good wholesome food – almonds, pistachios and cashew nuts – then we would pray with our hands stretched out, begging for forgiveness for our sins and being thankful for the day. My mother and I would both then blow our prayerful words over my father and on each other. She would offer the food to us both and, as she travelled throughout the house, blow prayers on the smoke of the incense stick, so that the devil left and we were harmonised by the holy prayers of the day.

My father, always in his casual T-shirt and joggers, would relax, moving his hands in the sign of the Holy Cross, muttering simple words to his God the father, the Son and the Holy Spirit. My mother always, at the same time of the morning, would have her finely combed, long, waist-length hair, straight but damp, as she would never miss her bathing first thing every day. And she always wore her very pale-coloured sari, always looking elegant and slender and always clean. My father bent the rules by bathing when he wanted, and wearing whatever he fancied. I would be dressed like him in the mornings but my hair had to look exactly like hers, not tied up or in a style, but combed out very straight.

These three months, every day without fail, we both dressed in our white saris and remained like that throughout the day. We did not go out as my mother had forbidden us. Our neighbours did our shopping, not that we needed much these days as we both ate very little during this period. No meals, or rather no large family meals, were cooked, nor did we actually sit at the family dining table. Charlie often brought food from home, or got a simple takeaway for us, and at times we made sandwiches.

These months were very strange, and seemed to linger on as if we had lived a thousand nights of doomed blindness and days that seemed the same – never-ending.

It was *12 January 1979* – fresh memories and still an *uncertain future*, but a day of reconciliation and acceptance. We had just finished our fish and chips, which Charlie had brought us and we sat, all three of us, on the sofa – Mother and I in white and Charlie in bright red. Charlie knew that Mother wanted to talk to me and so she deliberately stayed. She kept smiling at me, then at Mother, then me again.

'What is it, Charlie?' I asked.

'Your mother will explain.'

'Mama? Mama, hooray, is it really time for us to talk now?'

'Yes, of course, child, but I will do the talking while you listen.'

There seemed to be a softness to her voice. It made me feel that our last three months could be erased now and we could get back to normal. I could go back to school and play, yes play, with the boys outside our house. I knew that I would have to listen to her now and behave as she wanted, and of course grow up quickly, but that I had got accustomed to anyway.

'Tomorrow, child, will be the day when our new life will form properly. It may seem vague to you, but nevertheless, it is now our only future. You know, child, that no one can die with anyone; it is only when the good Lord wants it to happen that it can actually happen, that it actually will, so therefore we have to live in the best, dignified way possible.'

Clearing her throat, she carried on as if she was reading this message out to me, as if for the last few months she had practised these words in her head. Normally she would not talk to me in this tone, but because she was planning something that I might not like, her tone was different.

'Our long hair cannot be any more,' she continued, 'we have to get it cut off because I am a widow, and you… you an orphan.'

'But I still have you!'

'No, child, don't interrupt. And no, I may be alive but every child takes on the name of their father, never the mother. Also, we have to give our decorative clothes to charity as we both can no longer wear them, we can only wear plain clothes. Get used to not having your music, and if you do, no one else should hear it. You may watch television, but keep it low and appropriate. Your behaviour should be of a mature responsible girl, not the Sania we all know. There will be no make-up or jewellery until you are married, when really you will be set free. And yes, finally, every so often, you will need to fast for your father. You want him to be proud of you, don't you?'

'He was.'

'OK, but things are different now, so very different... so very, very different.'

'Mama?'

'Less of the questions please, child. Instead, try and listen more. You'll be rewarded, truly.'

'But, Mama—'

'I have just said less, that's what I meant. Now go to bed.'

I looked at her, very disappointed, because she gave the orders and I had to listen and obey without any clarification. She looked at me and shook her head disapprovingly, as if to say, 'you've let me down again'. She had said this so many times. I got up in anger and walked straight upstairs to my room. I banged the door shut and kicked it as hard as I possibly could.

I could see the sun shining through my curtains. Why hadn't the sun shone in months? I started to think back. Maybe it had, but I had not noticed. Was today the beginning of a brighter future? Why had I noticed it today? I looked back at the clock. It was eight o'clock. I could smell the incense stick lit in the house. Oh, Lord, how strongly they smelt. I knew my mother would be upset if I did not join her, but who cares? She didn't, so I wouldn't.

'Are you awake?' It was Charlie.

'Yes Charlie.'

'Your mother is calling you.'

'Tell Her Majesty I'm coming.'

As I entered the sitting room, there she was, in her white sari: long, black hair draped like the darkness of the night, crying at the shame of having to cut her hair, for she had never had it cut. The most she had had cut was a whisker chopped at the bottom. She always said it was sin to cut one's hair. She used to say that every follicle of hair you cut off, once you die, you will need to search for and pick up with your eyelashes. I always laughed and said that that should be fine for both of us as we both had long, luscious eyelashes. My remarks disappointed her very much.

A woman, dressed also in white, stood behind her with a very big pair of scissors. She recited some words that were beyond my own understanding, and then her long, heavy hair became a short, shoulder-length crop. Her tears, as I had never seen before, were still running with force; her anger could be felt in her loud cries. I ran to her to comfort her. She turned her gaze away from me. I went to grab the hair, but the lady told me to leave it alone. She swept the hair and then stood as my mother handed her some money. She was smiling, very pleased with her reward. Why was she rewarded? Was it for getting the worst haircut right, because, as I looked at my mother from all angles, she still crying loudly, I saw how butchered my mother's hair was.

Why was it she cried more today, in front of me, than when my father died? Was her hair a symbol of something that I, as a young child, did not know? Was I expected to react in the same manner? Maybe I was, but damn it, I wasn't going to be upset today because, for the first time, I was going to get my hair cut, and yes, it would definitely suit my joggers and trainers a whole lot more. I could not, however, show my excitement.

I stood there with a big smile on my face when I saw all the hair on the floor. It was almost as if my head became lighter, less of a burden. The woman with the big scissors disapproved of my smile and said words of shame, and tutted at me. I really did not care.

A few weeks had gone by but still the memories of my father seemed so fresh. My future seemed to be very stale. After arguing for weeks and weeks about wanting to go back to school, my mother would not listen or agree. Was I ever going back to school? Why was I made to stay home for months now? Why was I not allowed outside either? Was it because she did not want me to be seen by anyone?

It was a Thursday afternoon and, as I sat looking out of my window, I saw Samuel coming back from school. I quickly opened the window and put my finger to my lips to quieten him, and threw a piece of paper out to him. I waved goodbye and he went away quickly before my mother could see him.

He was a faithful friend and did exactly what the note asked him to. At two o'clock in the afternoon the following day there was a knock at the door by a stranger. I quickly opened it before she could stop me.

'Mama, it's for you.'

'Yes, hello, can I help?' said Mother.

'Yes, we have come in connection with your daughter.'

Mother turned to me. 'Sania, go upstairs while I talk to these people.'

I did not want to upset her too much so I started to go upstairs. I went halfway up, and then sat on the stair. I could hear them asking her why she had said I had gone abroad. Why had it been months since I had been at school or even been outside? What was happening and why?

I listened to her replies very carefully, as she explained with such emotion. She told them that when my father died I was too traumatised to return to school and needed a break, so she sent me back home to her family, where I was very happy. She then told them that I had only just got back, and in a few weeks would be back at school. She said I'd needed time to get used to life here again, without a father. She assured them that she had my best educational interests at heart and in next to no time I would be back at school, but needed more time.

I was so angry; their replies did not even begin to register in my ears any more. As I started to go downstairs I heard the front door shut. They had left.

'Mama, why the lies?' I implored.

'Shut up and listen, you stupid girl. How dare you?'

'Yes, I do dare. Why, what are you going to do? I only want to go to school, that's all.'

'You will, in a few days. Now get out of my sight.'

'Yes, yes, you stupid, stupid girl,' I muttered quietly. Her words from my mouth; she looked and rolled her eyes.

The next few days were very quiet but I had got used to that. It was a Wednesday morning while we were both having our breakfast when the doorbell rang again. As I watched the yolk of my egg dripping from my toast, I knew it was about school again. Deep down inside I was happy as I had got the ball rolling and felt one day she would have to give in and let me go back to school. After all, that's all I wanted. I wanted my environment, to get back to how it used to be, not how it was at the moment. I felt it would also help me to forget about my father a little as I would be busy at school with my friends. I was a child and so naïve; she was the adult and so cunning. My dream was my school; her dream was a faraway destination, a land unknown to me, where everyone was a total stranger. Is that what the Lord had written for me?

A Holiday That Lasted a Lifetime

IT WASN'T THE good Lord who had written it for me, it was inscribed into my life by my mother, like lines marked into your palm and read by wise ones who decide your fate once they look at your hand. Fate or destiny, they are both the same thing – no wise man or words of wisdom by anyone. Her thoughts were her own, and I could not make any impression on them. Not even the thoughts she said out loud, let alone the search deep down for heartfelt answers. It was almost as if every time I looked at her, she looked, and as soon as she started to mellow, she would look away and take control of the situation. But what was the situation?

When it gets cold and dark we draw the curtains on the closed windows to keep everything out that we don't want to see any more and embrace our own small comforts of the warm radiator and the soft lighting. We can ignore the outside by creating a man-made false reality away from the real world out there. That feeling of her being inside, in the warm, in the lights, in her own man-made environment, and me, well, I was now a stranger to all that. I was the stranger who no one let in. That's how I felt.

A week had gone by and it was Friday once more. Today, Mama's mood seemed much better. On her awakening she seemed to acknowledge the fact that I existed. I should have known that there had to be a reason, but how naïve I was. She explained that after breakfast she had something very important to explain to me and a decision that she had made that was right for us both. Today she made a lavish breakfast for us both and we sat together and ate our meal.

She quickly tidied up as I remained in my breakfast chair. She sat opposite me and looked right into my eyes. She explained how she was not coping and how she needed a break away from the constant memories of my father, the death and the funeral. While she carried on I was actually amazed, but also very disturbed, because it was the very first time she said that he was dead, or even mentioned him or the funeral. In a way it comforted me to know that she had now opened up and admitted to the harsh reality of life. Her final words were, 'Please child, believe me when I say that we both need this break, especially me, to get over this tragedy.'

'Where are we going?' I asked.

'We will go to India and stay for a few weeks. The different environment, fresh food and fresh air of the countryside will do us a lot of good. Anyway, maybe seeing my family is just what I need.'

'Do you promise that we will be back soon and then I can go back to school?'

'Of course, my love. Have I ever stopped you from going to school?'

'Well, not before, but now you have.'

'But child, you do not understand my trauma, how depressed I have become. That's why. I could not let you out of my sight.'

'OK, Mama.'

'Great, well, in that case, we shall go tomorrow.'

'Tomorrow, Mama? How can we go so quickly?' I said with great surprise. 'Don't you think you should've asked me before making arrangements? What if I'd said no?'

'My child, I knew you would never let me down!'

As we got our passports back from the immigration control in India, Mother kept looking around, eagerly trying to see her family. Then, all of a sudden, she waved and swayed her head, laughing, her eyes filled with joyful tears. She let go of the baggage trolley and I kept total command of it while she kissed and hugged her family. For a short while I felt that maybe it was good that we came because she was happy, and it was nice to see her this way after such a long time. She held my hand and we walked towards a taxi. We all got in. There were seven of us in the taxi. They all kissed and hugged her, but no one did that to me. Was I not anything to them? Was I not her daughter? I knew I had my father's skin colour but I had my mother's looks, hair and body. Wasn't that enough for them?

I kept looking at all of them as they squashed next to each other to fit into one taxi. They did not look back at me. I whispered to my mother, asking her why they were ignoring me. She replied that it was because they did not know me.

The scenery towards the small village was very beautiful. The town smelt greatly of traffic and car fumes, but then the town's hustle and bustle faded as we approached the villages.

We arrived at our destination. A big gate opened and our cases got taken in. We both followed everyone. There was lots of open space in the middle of the courtyard, and this was surrounded by houses. Wooden beds with rope-woven mattresses were laid out for all to sit on. Women, looking dowdy and dressed in traditional clothing, were behaving in a very proper manner, probably on their best behaviour in front of all the guests. Lots of women were sitting together on the wooden beds, chatting and gossiping about families. Men were sitting separately to the women. They chatted to one another about work, animals and the price of meat at the bazaar. As I watched the men, somehow the young ones looked all alike, and thinking carefully about it, so did the older men. The young ones were all skinny and had greasy hair; the old ones were all wrinkly, with at least one tooth missing and all with dark skins and even darker moustaches. Why is it that they all had a moustache? This was the symbol of masculinity, I later found out.

There was one thing that was the same for the men and the women, and that was their clothes. They all wore *shalwar kameez*. To us Westerners it's like trousers with a shirt. Women had their heads covered with shawls or *dupattas*, which are like scarves. Men had a bundle of white cloth around their heads or on the shoulders. I think it would be fair to say that no matter what age or sex, there was a distinctive smell of sweat and heat they all shared – it was so strong and almost embedded in their clothes. I later also realised the clothes were only changed on average once or twice a week.

Meat was being cooked on the earthen stones and the open, clay oven had the smell of fresh bread being baked. The curry smell was strong, but almost nice; somehow a fresher kind of smell. A young man, almost an Elvis Presley lookalike in hairstyle only, came over with a small, half-stable coffee table and placed it by our legs. The young girls all brought food onto the table and told us to start eating.

We both got up to go and wash our hands when, quickly, one of the women said, 'No, no. Don't get up. We are bringing the water for you to wash your hands with. Hurry, girlie.'

In an instant, a girl came with a jug of water and poured it on our hands. She offered us her scarf with which to dry our hands.

She was the first to actually smile at me. It was so nice to see that, maybe, she would become a friend to me. I really hoped so. Everyone was a stranger, and my mother, well, she was still acting like a stranger even though she shouldn't have, especially not here. We ate at the table but my mother insisted that someone should join us, so a few of them did. The rest sat on small, nearly flat, stools on the floor, very close to the clay fire. As they all ate, they threw bones onto the floor. My mother and I kept them on our plates. The men finished before the women. They ate more but also ate at great speed, and then they took a glass of water, swirled the water around in their mouths making obscene noises, and spat out the mouthful near where they were sitting. What a lovely mouthwash!

As they spat or threw their bones, the cockerels came running in a hope of getting some leftovers. Some of the boys sat looking between their legs, because that's where their plate was – on the floor – but with a shy glance would keep looking at me whenever they got the chance, which was when the older ones were not looking at them. I was almost beside myself with shock at their table manners – when they finished they wiped their mouths with their sleeves and their hands on their shirts.

The rest of the afternoon was almost a daze as I was very tired after the flight. An eight-hour night flight with no sleep was just too bad. I had gone to the toilet on the aeroplane, which was just as well, because after my meal I needed to use the toilet again. The old woman told one of the young girls to show me the new toilet that they recently had installed. A privilege, they said, and just in time for us *goreh*, meaning white ones. I followed her and she led me to a cubicle. She stood there, looking at me. I looked back and asked, 'Where is the toilet?'

'There, look,' she replied.

'Where?'

'Go forward and look.'

Then I saw it. There was a flat pan dug into the floor where you would squat and empty your insides – whether from the mouth or the backside because, believe me, there was such a stink.

I then asked, 'How will I flush the toilet?'

'Flush? What's that? You use the tap and the jug and pour water into the toilet until it all goes down.'

'Don't you have another one, an English one?'

'You don't like this one?'

'No.'

'OK, I'll show you what we all use.'

'Great.'

She led and I followed. We walked out of the courtyard and along the alley which took us to their graveyard, and out onto their land. The scenery was certainly beautiful, but also smelly – there was excrement scattered around; some dry, some wet, some human, some animal.

'Where would you like to do it?' she asked.

'Do what?'

'You said you wanted to go for a shit?'

'No, I didn't.'

'All right, for a wee then.'

'Yes, I do.'

'Well go on then, anywhere you like. I'll keep watch.'

'Watch from whom?'

'Well from people obviously. You'll know when the animals are coming.'

'Won't my clothes get wet?'

'Yes, that's why we rarely wear a sari, only for going out in. *Shalwar kameez* is better – less fabric, less to hold onto.'

'But won't my feet get wet?'

'Well, you're a real madam, a *gori* madam. Either you get used to getting wet or you'll learn like us.'

'What do you mean by that?'

'We don't have a choice, whether it's a number one or number two. You need to do it, or you get wet. Only you can make the choice, but whichever one, pick a stone that is free from mud and round.'

'What do you mean?'

'What do I mean? Aren't you going to clean yourself?' the girl asked indignantly.

'I thought I would use the tissue in my hand.'

'And how long is that going to last, Madam?'

I stared at her for a long time and it was difficult to contest – a choice without a choice really. Parade naked in the open air or be suffocated by smell while squatting so the fumes go straight up your nose.

Well, which is it going to be, Sania? I thought. My mind was in turmoil, my bladder anxious.

'Here,' I said.

'Go on then, anywhere you like, I'll keep watch.'

I quickly realised that I needed to sit with my legs much further apart than I had anticipated, as my feet started to get a little wet. Very un-ladylike, I must say.

Along with the food being different, the sleeping arrangements were different too; we all slept in the same big room. All day was spent sitting with visitors. At least everyone started to be a bit friendlier, especially with Mama. She seemed really happy. The cultural shock was tremendous but I didn't moan just to see her happy.

A month had gone by and I asked Mama when we were going to go back. She simply replied, 'A little longer.'

Things seemed to be a bit busy one day while I was still asleep. Food was being cooked early and a special dish called *halwa* – a sweet semolina dish – was being made. I asked Maansi, my faithful lavatory attendant, what was going on. She told me to ask Mama. I went to find her, but could not hear or see her. Finally, there was only one room that I had not been in, the guest room. I knocked and went in. I stood there, still and very silent. She sat there in the middle of the bed, dressed in a colourful sari; a red wedding scarf was lying beside her. There were boxes of jewellery beside her also. She had henna on her hands and feet, and red lipstick, which she had not worn in a very long time. How could this be true? Was I seeing right? I stood still, silent and shocked. She looked just like she did in the photo that is displayed in our own house, but with my father. I knew then that this *holiday was going to last a lifetime.*

A Disillusioned New Beginning

SHE CALLED ME so many times and her voice kept ringing in my ears for a long time. I didn't reply; there was only silence. I walked away, leaving the door ajar, in a state of shock. I went to our sleeping room and sat on my bed, sobbing with all my might. No one took any notice, and yet everyone heard. Were they expecting this reaction? No one comforted me. I sat all alone, weeping, pouring out my heart in silence. My tears told my pain but my words just could not come out. I heard a small commotion and people entered the garden area. A mat was laid outside the room and they all sat on it. I kept looking for a groom but I couldn't see one. I moved closer just in case I was wrong.

A priest started to recite some holy words and the fire in the middle was burning the fury of my heart even though it was tiny, nothing like a real wedding fire. Soon she stepped out and someone tied her scarf to a man's scarf. He walked, leading her. She followed with her head down. So she should – full of shame – but that's me talking and not her. She reached down and touched his feet, and he stood smiling like a toothless goon.

They now sat together. She did not even try to look at me, otherwise she would have seen the weeping child, her child, all alone. Maansi saw me. She came over to rub it in even further by saying that this was no longer our house. I had to go with Mother to our new home. But I had not even got used to regarding this one as my own home, even after a month. How could I be uprooted again? I calmed myself down with the knowledge that soon we would be going back to the UK, and I would get back to as near to normal as possible. She could do what she liked, after all, it's not as if she really cared.

Everyone was seated on the floor. The women served while all the men ate. The women gathered around the clay fire and ate as they normally would have, including the female guests. 'Come and eat, Sania,' someone said. 'You can't stay hungry.'

I was not hungry. I stayed in the same room watching everyone. The men were having their tea now, and talking about all kinds of things. The women were washing and cleaning while gossiping about families and who's done what with whom. I was all alone, all by myself. First there were three of us, then two lonely women and now there was only one and that was me: very lonely, all alone, poor me…

I was told to follow my mother to our new home and, like a good girl, that's what I did. After all, it was pretty clear that they didn't want me to stay with them anyway. Our walk was not very far. In fact, it was just around the corner. We entered a gate and inside was a shamble of a house. There were only four rooms here. A buffalo was standing right in the middle of the garden, and there were lambs and goats scattered everywhere. All I could see was the faeces of all the animals and the smell of their existence all around.

I walked into my new life helpless, unloved, uncared for, but most of all, not even thought of. Why is it that no one, not even my mother, had bothered to tell me about the wedding? Moreover, she really should have asked me. After all, it involved me as well, didn't it? How could she replace my father, the man we both loved?

He walked in front, and the rest of the few guests, including me, followed into the main sitting room. Mother stood just outside and then she delicately spilled rice from the clay bowl with her dainty, beautiful feet – a sign made by

45

all new brides to bring prosperity into the new life. Everyone sat down and *mitai* – sweet meats – were handed around. Everyone tucked in as if they had never had this delicacy before. Looking at their faces, so full of hunger and greed, it did not really surprise me. Slowly they all started to leave and soon there was only this new family here; she and I had both become a part of it.

Some members of the family started to do the cooking, as everyone here in India seemed to eat just before dark due to the fact that only some homes had electricity. Those fortunate enough to have it still had spells of power cuts as the local government tried to cut costs and save energy. One woman sat with Mother and I sat opposite her, all the while looking straight at her. She never once looked in my direction or returned my stare. The woman told us both to go into Mother's new room and relax, as it had been a long day, reminding her that her new husband would be in after everyone had eaten; Mother had a little time to sleep, relax or unwind. She led us both into a small room, which was really the kitchen, but they had taken the clay fire holder out and replaced it with a bed. It was decorated with tacky tinsel, and on the bed there was a disgusting, red coloured sheet with flower petals all over it. What a romantic scene, or so it should have been, but why, why did she have to be the bride?

We both sat on the bed and the woman left. She quickly moved her hand to touch mine, and I moved mine onto my lap. She then brought her hand onto my lap.

'Don't you dare ever touch me again,' I snapped.

'Why, Sania, why?'

'Why? You're the bride; you should have the answers.'

'Look, it was never my idea,' she said, trying to explain. 'It was just to keep my mother happy, for she said that she never saw my wedding to your father and always wished to see her daughter, her only child, a bride. That's why. I couldn't refuse, could I now, Sania?'

'And you never thought of telling me?'

'Well, I did, but I knew you'd be like this!'

'What is "like this"? How the hell do you expect me to be? Am I supposed to be happy for you and congratulate you on this auspicious occasion? For heaven's sake, look at you – a mother of a teenager and getting married, and worst of all, not ever telling me, your own flesh and blood. How could you, how could you?'

I was crying hysterically by this point. She tried to calm me down, only so that the others could not hear, but I did not care. She tried to touch me, but there was no way that I would have that either. I cried my lonely tears, all alone, no one to share them with, no one listened or cared. They soon dried up and I was quiet again. We both sat in silence. This was never going to work; it was *a disillusioned new beginning.*

We had been sitting in the one position for hours. Suddenly a girl much older than me came in and said, 'Mother, dear, come and eat. Oh and of course, you too, little sister.'

'Mother dear? How dare you, you bitch,' I said furiously to the girl. 'She is only my mother. I am her only child. How dare you? Anyway, she can't be a good mother to me so how can she be a mother to you, you stupid, stupid girl? …Oh no, that's me.'

'Please don't be upset,' responded the girl. 'What would you rather I call her? She is my uncle's new wife, and he is a father figure to me. It is up to me to respect her, she is my elder.'

'Oh, just shut up and get lost you bitch.'

Mother intervened. 'Sania, get a grip of yourself, child. What are you doing? It's not her fault.'

'How dare you blame me!' With that I rushed off the bed and charged at the girl, slapping her and pulling her hair, all the while telling her that I would kill her. My mother got up and tore us apart, and told the girl to go. She quickly left without uttering a word. I ran into the big room. It was empty except for six beds that were placed with sheets on them. This was obviously the sleeping room. For the night only though, because I had to quickly learn that during the day the bedroom turned into a sitting room. I lay on the bed that was right next to the window, listening for any conversation, but I could not clearly understand what anyone was saying. Tears ran from my eyes, onto my nose and straight into my mouth from my right eye, and tears from the left made a small pool near my face.

As the darkness of the night arrived, so did she, into her room, followed by him, his mouth closed, his fingers rubbing along the moustache on his face and smiling as he closed the door. I felt so hurt and sick, my eyes sore, my face raging with anger almost to the point where I could feel my blood boil. I got up from the bed and stormed into their room; they were both smiling, cuddling each other, with his ugly black face on hers, his moustache caressing her cheek.

As they looked at me they pulled the sheet on them to cover themselves. I went to him and started to pull his hair, and boy, did he have lots. The more I pulled, the more that came out in my hand.

'Get off her, you bastard. Get off, get off, she's my dad's, no one else's! Get off, get off—'

'Oh, someone take this hysterical girl away before I shoot her dead. She doesn't know me yet or else she would never have challenged me.'

As soon as he finished saying that, another man came and grabbed me by the waist and carried me to where I was supposed to sleep. I tried to break free but to no avail. He threw me on the bed nearest the door. I lay there, silent. He then smiled and said, 'Do you want me to show you what a man is all about? After all, why go to him when there's me? Shall I show you my manhood? Gagging for it are you? Are you a virgin? Are you new?'

For the first time in my life I was actually scared of the opposite sex. I quietly replied, 'No, what?'

He watched over me for quite a while, twisting his moustache with his hands and rubbing his lips. He then licked his lips slowly, as I swallowed the lump in my throat, afraid, so afraid. All I could think at this moment was that if my father were alive this would not be happening. Moreover I would not be afraid. He arched his eyebrows at me, smiled with his eyes, turned around and left the room. I breathed a sigh of relief. My heart was pounding so very fast. I began to calm down as I started to regret my own actions today, and how I nearly got myself into a situation that maybe I had brought on myself. What if he had done something? Furthermore, what if he had done what he said?

Looking back on it now, I realise that as a young girl I should never have put myself in that situation, for it could have been traumatic for me, but at that time I blamed her completely – if she had not got married to him, I would not have rebelled. Why did she do that without even mentioning it to me? I felt stupid as well, stupid and naïve. How come everyone knew, or seemed to know, what was happening except me?

I know that I had grown attached to Maansi since our first date in search of the perfect position and location to empty my bladder. Somehow she found it hilarious that a madam, as she called me, had to resort to such a life. She did tell me that the luxuries that I was used to had to remain back in England. We used to sleep with our beds next to each other. We always went to the toilet together and ate our meals together. Maybe that's why my mother had all the time to prepare for her new life, a new beginning? Maybe what she didn't realise was that this was to be a new beginning for me and was forced upon me. Was it the same for her? No, it could not be. She was the adult, I was the child; she had the choice, I did not.

All I thought that night was, *How could she? What did this all mean? Is he going to step into my father's shoes, or dress in his clothes, and have privileges like driving his car?* But more so, where was he going to sleep? I did not need to think long on that as I had already seen first-hand. She betrayed me, that is all I could really see and I believed it. All night long, that picture of his grubby, dirty black hands on her shoulder, his face next to hers came back to me. It was disgusting and made me feel sick.

I cannot remember what time I dozed off, but I know that the others in the house came and slept in the same room. I kept my window open. It was dark; you could see very little, even though the lanterns were still lit and they were powerful. We did not have any electricity, so oil lanterns or big torches were used. The big torch was put outside her bedroom so that if she got up there would still be light for her. Soon the three lights were turned off and it was pitch black. My eyes could see no more.

I really did not know what time it was but it was still very dark outside and I was really desperate to go for a wee. There was no light outside. I did not know where the lantern was any more. I didn't really know my way around the house or the garden. I suppose it was my own fault really, because in the heat of my own fury I forgot to go to the toilet, and here in India you cannot forget to go in time. Everything is on time: chores get done before dark and you get up at sunrise. I was feeling really uncomfortable, so I rolled onto my side and kept my eyes shut real tight, hoping to doze off. It did not work. I got up, pulled my flip-flops on (I was still in my wedding day clothes) and headed off to the garden. I left the door ajar behind me just in case something happened to me; they would hear.

I remembered how, when the women washed the dishes – believe me only the women did, never men – they always threw the dirty water in the direction of the gate because this is where there was a small ditch running away; the water would run out of the garden all the way to the gate, and into the alley where people walk. They wash dishes in this house, so they must have a ditch as well, I thought. If I did a wee here no one would really know. I certainly could not go out or use the toilet as I did not know of its whereabouts. But anyway, it was fine as no one would know anyway.

I got back into bed, shutting the door behind me. I fell asleep straight away.

I could hear the cockerel even though I was so tired. Gradually the light turned into sunshine and the goats started bleating. I could smell and hear the buffalo busily emptying her bladder while swinging her tail so that it spread everywhere.

I opened my eyes to see through the wooden window. It was shut, but I had left it open. Someone shut it purposely. I looked around. No one was in the room. I was all alone. Angrily, I opened the window and watched, with my head still on the hard pillow. There she was, in her new glad rags, sitting on the bed outside, almost posing like a new bride. She sat there drying her hair with the towel. Aren't these things meant to be private? She didn't have a sari on. She wore a *shalwar kameez*; now she looked just like the other women here. I could feel my temperature rise as I kept staring at her. She was unaware that I was watching her. Had she no shame? In her religion, after a man and woman 'get together', for those were the words used for sex, they always had to wash themselves from top to toe and recite a prayer. I knew about this as my father and her would both get up and wash each morning, sometimes together and other times separately, but at times my father, especially if running late for work, would not. My mother would subtly say, 'You are creating a sin,' thinking that I was unaware of what she meant. He was not of her religion so he did not care. How could she sit there after her wash today? She was telling everyone that they had become one, a man and a woman, showing the world – that included me.

The old woman came in and told me to get up or I'd miss breakfast. *Who cares*, I thought, because breakfast was tea and rusks or *parathas*. Breakfast for me was bread, eggs and cereal, not tea rusks. I ignored her and carried on watching. Deep down inside I knew the real reason why I did not want to get up. I did not know what this new day had in store for me after the shock I had the day before. Somehow I felt that if I stayed in bed all day I could ignore the day, but that was a myth as I saw her coming towards me. I knew it was time for a confrontation again. My thoughts raced: What am I going to say to her and how? What will she say to me? And more to the point, how will I react to seeing her and listening to her give me explanations, making pathetic excuses for herself, trying to convince me that life would be better now and how she was doing all this for me? I know her. But really it was too late for explanations as the damage had already been done: the reasoning meant nothing.

Tears of Betrayal

MANY WEEKS HAD gone by in this new beginning, this new life that she made for both of us. She had been offering small lectures, all starting with a few sorrowful words, about our new life and how a father figure was very important for my upbringing, and the end always being how I had to accept that this was the way it had to be. I could not agree with any word of hers and really, you could say, we were at logger-heads with one another. Even though we had many words together, we never really talked to each other in a calm, relaxed manner, but I knew that I had to do this, for I needed to know when this holiday was going to end and I could go back home.

I could have calmed myself but the problem was him. He was always there like a bad smell and every time I tried to get her by herself to talk, he would arrive just in the nick of time, almost as if trying to prevent her from talking openly to me. Why couldn't he let a mother and her daughter talk alone? Because of the lack of communication, lack of love and a horrible feeling of being unwanted, I felt that I was becoming more and more depressed. I say that with great regret as I used to be a happy child and had not known being sad or depressed.

I was allowed to go to my grandmother's house, my mama's mother – Beeji, as they called her – and, even though they – the elders especially – were not very friendly with me, as least I was made welcome by the youngsters, particularly Maansi. She was only two years older than I was but had never been to school – she had to look after the children and the house while her mother tended to the animals and the older generation. She said she had been cooking and cleaning since the age of eight, and had had some education from her younger sister who did go to school. She was like a mother figure to both her brother and sister.

She knew that I was not happy and would always ask, 'What is it, Madam? Why are you looking so sad?' Even though I had explained everything in full to her, she was never amazed or shocked. She would say, 'Well, Madam, it happens here all the time. It's normal life. Just imagine, my mother was married at the age of twelve, and at your age she had already had me. I would have been the same if it hadn't been for the fact that the man I was supposed to marry went off to England in search of work. So I could say that I am also very lucky. As for you, Sania Madam, you don't know how good you've got it.'

This conversation was very repetitive as I tended to go to her nearly every day. She had also told me that I had to accept the fact that he was my new dad, and act like his child. She said that rebelling against him would only cause more trouble. I told her firmly that that was not going to happen, for my mother and I had only come for a holiday and would be going back soon. She laughed at me and replied, 'How naïve you are, Madam. Hasn't your education ever taught you about real life? This is not your holiday, this is your home. Grandma told us and, you know, she is the head of the house and she knows what's what.'

These words kept ringing in my ears, 'this is your home…' I kept staring at her, annoyed, upset and very angry at the deceit. Tears just would not stop, but I really did not want to cry in front of her; I just could not stop myself. She said she was sorry for upsetting me, but it was the truth, and she couldn't understand why I was upset. She should have understood it was because I had a different life to hers.

I stormed out and went home. As I entered the gate I saw my mother sitting on a small, wooden stool, which everyone used rather than sitting on the bare, concrete floor. He was sitting right next to her rolling his moustache, acting like a lovesick dog. And I use the word 'dog' because his other hand was on his private parts, rubbing them also. As soon as they saw me, the smile went from her face and he stopped his disgusting actions.

Earlier that morning, I had gone over to Maansi's in the hope that I would become relaxed and then be able to come back and talk to Mother calmly, urging her to let us both go back home. But, as always, things had not gone to plan. I was still in tears, my face raging with anger and I was embarrassed at being lied to.

'Can I talk to you, Mama, in private please?'

'Yes, of course,' Mother answered.

'No, no one is going anywhere,' he interrupted. 'Whatever you both want to say has to be said here. A woman cannot have any conversations in private; nothing is private from a husband or father. Say whatever you need to in front of me.'

'When are we going back?' I said. 'Someone told me that we are not going back. Please tell me, Mama, that that is a lie. I'm dying to go back home as soon as possible. I hate it here.'

He interrupted, 'Hate it here? I have provided a roof over your heads and food in your stomachs. I have also done a big deed by marrying a widow, your mother, and you are not grateful? Instead you say you hate it.'

'Please calm down, both of you,' said Mother.

'Don't you tell your husband to calm down. A woman doesn't ever answer back to her husband or go against his wishes. You have to honour every wish of your husband, didn't I tell you the very first night? Didn't it sink in the first time, or do I need to reinforce it again? If I do, it won't be nicely; it will be with the back of my hand. That is the only way to handle women after all. They don't have brains. They just follow the man and respect his wishes. Those who live in the shadow of a man are true women in the Indian society.'

'All right, I understand. I'm sorry, please, I'm sorry,' she begged.

'Mama, you would never have taken anything from Papa, but then he would definitely not have said anything like this. He would never speak to you like this. Why are you letting him talk to you in this way?'

'Things are different now, child, as you now have to respect your father and listen to him.'

'He is not my father and he never will be.'

'Calm down, child, please.'

'Oh, you bitch of a girl,' he butted in angrily. 'Don't ever speak to your mother like this or else I will have to discipline you as well. After all, ask your mother, I sorted her out. Do you need sorting?'

'I can sort myself out, thank you,' I retorted. 'Anyway, you are no one to me so I don't have to listen to you—'

Before I could finish my sentence he had grabbed me by the hair and dragged me onto the floor. I sat flat on the floor, his knee on my lap and a firm grip on my hair. I held my head, which was pulled back by him, in my hands, in pain and now uttering new words. His face, or rather his moustache, was so close to my face that while he was talking and hurling swear words, his spit flew at me. Tears ran from my eyes, but I made no sound; silent tears, tears of silence.

My mother came down to me and, kneeling, told him that I would behave and to let me go. He lashed out and slapped her straight across her face with his spare hand. She wept, her hand covering where he had hit her. She sat helpless next to me, crying.

'Is the tea ready yet, Daughter-in-law?' said his mother. We all looked in the direction of where the voice was coming from. She stood next to us now.

'Why are you doing this, son? What has happened?'

'Never you mind, and anyway it has nothing to do with you or anyone else, so go back inside.'

'Please, Dev, don't do this. I'm telling you this for your own good. Just think of others for once rather than yourself. Your first wife Khushi certainly lived up and still lives up to her name – Happy – for that is her. She eats and sleeps here, obeys every whim of yours and still utters no word. Is this what you want out of your life?'

'Get lost, Mother,' he spat out. 'I've told you already, and anyway I've heard all this before.'

'Please, Dev, let go of the child, poor, helpless child.' She pulled his hands off my hair. He stood there fuming.

'Why are you protecting her? What is she to you?'

'She is your second wife's daughter and therefore my only step-grandchild.'

'She's not mine so I don't have any blood ties with her. I can do what I like.'

'Blood ties? You're lucky you have a stepchild. You have never been blessed with a child. Look at yourself. No wonder God never blessed you with any children. He knew what you were like.'

'Just shut up and go inside, Mother, and mind your own business, meddling cow.'

With this she turned her back, looking really hurt, and walked off into the sitting room. I ran into the bedroom, onto my bed, and lay there looking at the ceiling while tears dripped from the corners of my eyes into my scalp. My nose was running onto my lips and onto my chin. I grabbed the sheet that I was lying on and wiped it away. We had no tissues.

'Brother, why don't you go to the bazaar, have some tea and smoke a lot, that'll help you relax. Go on.'

I looked out of the window. His younger brother, Anil, who they all called Chotu, was calming him down. They seemed so different from one another. Anil always wore *shalwar kameez* like all the rest of us, as these are worn by both sexes. But Dev, he always dressed so typically 'village' in style. He always wore a *thothi*, which is like a wrap-around skirt, tied at the waist, like a sheet wrapped around with a vest on the top. He hurriedly ran towards the gate. My mama was still sitting on the floor, sobbing.

In spite of everything she had done to me, I actually felt sorry for her. I quickly ran to her. Naturally I asked her to stop crying as I put my arms around her, and asked her the one question I wanted an answer to – when were we going home? It was the first time ever, since we came, that she talked to me nicely and calmly. There was the love that she, for the first time in so long, showered on me. She smiled and looked into my eyes, and talked like a real mother once again. It was as if I had found my long-lost mother again. It was such a nice feeling that I had completely forgotten my question.

She went on to explain how her mother's family resented me because I was a white man's child. Not just that but the fact that she had married against their will and now, in her hour of need, turned up here. She said that if her father was alive he wouldn't have allowed her in the house, but since he was no longer alive, her mother was more accepting, but on her conditions. She had to marry someone from here, someone of the same religion, caste and culture. She accepted it because she said she needed the very little family she had.

I asked her why the elders stopped the youngsters from talking to me. What had I done? They even told Maansi not to be over-friendly, but she ignored them. In reply she said that the elders, including her mother, did not believe that she had had a Hindu marriage with my father. How could an Englishman possibly have a Hindu marriage? After all, he was not Hindu; where was the proof? So, in their eyes, she went on to explain, I was born out of wedlock, and therefore I was an illegitimate child – a bastard child.

My life was not that unbearable really, because, even though Grandmother Beeji, the eldest member of the family, was a bit hostile towards me, Beeji's youngest brother Zaif was quite nice to me when no one was looking. As for his wife, Huma, well, she did not like the look of me, and I would hear her tell Maansi and the younger two, Madi and Manoo, to keep away from the white people as they were different. I think she was just jealous because I was fair; in fact, as English as anyone else really. Often, when she saw me after a shower, she would make strange grimaces, and say to her two youngest things like, 'Why can't you wash yourself well? Why don't you look clean?'

I know that if Beeji had accepted me, then everyone else would have as well. She ruled the house as she was the eldest and everyone respected her totally. No one called her by her name – Mittali – as Beeji was a respectable word for mother.

As for this new house, my mama's husband, Dev, Anil, the nice younger brother with his new wife, Dina, Dev's first wife, Khushi, and the gruesome man who almost assaulted me the night of Mama's wedding, lived in it. I knew that Badi Ma (big mother) was something of a grandmother figure here; she had the same respect and status as Beeji. I reflected and thought in silence.

'So, when are we going back home, Mama?' I asked her.

'Back home? Well, I don't know, child. I suppose when they allow me to.'

'Who?'

'Well, Dev of course.'

'And who else? You said they.'

' "They" is the respectful way of talking about a husband.'

'But you never called Papa that.'

'I know, but Dev told me that he wanted to be called nothing less than that on the very first night, along with telling me how to behave.'

'You know what, we could run away, both of us, go to the airport and board the plane back home.'

'Do you even know where the airport is? We have lived in one house and then been transported into this house. We have never left this village, let alone seen a town or the airport. And we need passports to board a plane, and money for tickets, which I don't have.'

'I'm sure we could borrow some money or I'll steal some; you just have the passports ready!'

'No can do, child, it's not that simple, for he took the passports from me on our wedding night.'

'And?'

'And,' she continued, 'I have not seen them since. I've searched and asked, but no luck.'

'Oh, God!' I started crying, loudly, again. Mama was trying to calm me down all the while. Her cries fell on deaf ears as I was trying to come to terms with this grand new life of ours. Why, oh why, did it have to happen to me? I could not imagine myself living here much longer, but now I realised there was no means of escape, none that I could see anyway; it was like living on death row where your fate was in someone else's hands. I felt like we were living on a different planet. I just wanted my old life and home back.

'If only Papa was alive,' I lamented.

'Yes, if only,' said Mama, 'but please don't cry. Save your tears, child.'

'What do you mean by that? The reason why we are stuck here is you. Have you no sense? Why are you being pushed around? You weren't like that before, not back home.'

Mama was silent.

'I'll save my tears, but for more betrayal,' I added angrily.

'My life was different then,' she said, trying to explain, 'I was a different person then.'

'No, you're the same person, except your head has gone to graze.'

No reply.

I got up and went to lie on my bed, looking through the window, observing and thinking as hard as my young mind would allow me to. I knew I had to do something, but I also knew that I could get killed by this man; he was violent, bad tempered and despicably rude. He had a rifle hung over his bed, which he used to kill birds while they flew over the house. He never missed. I knew that I had to get someone on side, as he never left the house – someone whom I could get money from. I would steal some, but where would I get my hands on thousands of rupees? Where, how and who?

This holiday was lasting a lifetime!

Errors of Innocence

TWO WEEKS HAD gone by and, as to our plan, Mother started asking Dev for a little money for her private things: toiletries, make-up, perfume and clothes. You could tell that she was not using money on new products, but every time he questioned her about the money he'd given and where she'd spent it, she would always reply that he wanted her to look her best at all times and it cost money to look good.

She didn't look good but, being a backward, uneducated man, he knew no better. So long as she had bright-red lipstick on, and her cleavage showed, he thought she had spent time and money to look that way. I suppose, compared to the rest of the village women, she did look good. Maybe a bit over the top, but she had a mission to accomplish.

I was amazed that she would stoop so low, but then she had never been so helpless before. She was modest in every way, but now, in this new persona, no trace of modesty could be found. She would often stand inside her doorway and lure him in by beckoning him with her finger. He would sit and enjoy the attention, then, clearing his throat with excitement, he would start rubbing his chest, and in no time his hands would be on his private parts. Why is it that no one said anything to him while he did this in front of them? Are all the men here desperate like him? I think the women just felt embarrassed when he did that, so mentioned nothing or just ignored him.

He would walk so upright, with shoulders thrown back, as if he were on some important mission. I hated him for his actions but hated her more for what she was doing. But she kept convincing me that it was the only way she could get money and maybe the passports. How could I stoop so low? But then, I was desperate too!

She had to carry on playing her games as she had only secured 200 rupees from him in two weeks, which was far from what we needed to purchase airline tickets. Maansi knew my plan, and though she said I would never get away with it, she was very excited. As she said, it was like a movie plot with all the secrets, thrills and lies. How did she know about movies? She said that she had watched a few on someone else's television and video machine, she had heard plays and dramas on her father's radio, and learnt about movies on a show called *Bombay Talkies*. Many people would come over to listen to it. The men here mostly enjoyed listening to the cricket commentary.

She also helped by giving me money she had saved from her 'sweets' allowance (they never had regular pocket money). She said she had twenty-five rupees for me. I was so grateful to her, for she did not have to help at all. This money was so little for my needs, and yet for her it was a great amount. She said she would help me in our great escape. She knew the danger, but still she was so excited. As for me, I think I was more scared.

I had done my part also. I had asked Auntie Khushi, whom I called Moti Masi, Dev's first wife, for money, and told her that I desperately needed it. She said she had money in her joint account with her husband – money he had given her – but she was not allowed to go to the bazaar or the bank on her own. However, he would never question her needs for money. She did say that she had some at home and could give me that when I needed it. She said that most of the money she got now was not from her husband, but given by her parents, brothers and others from her side of the family when they came to visit. It is not customary to come and dine at your daughter's house. Usually they would go to eat elsewhere. There had been the odd occasion when they would eat lunch at Khushi's though, for which they would reward her with money. Her husband had never taken this money away, and she had not had a real use for it either.

Every time I looked at her it made me smile, for she was always smiling. Also, don't they say that fat people are always happy? This applied to her very well. I couldn't understand how she could remain positive and happy. Dev was never loving towards her, and yet she did everything he asked her to: clean this, get that, make this. He never exchanged any feelings with her like he did with my mother. She was still his wife and of course he kept reminding her of that. Auntie Khushi and I ate our meals together with Badi Ma, Uncle Anil and his wife, Auntie Dina, while Mama and Dev ate together – always by the open fire. The gruesome animal that had frightened me so much on that first night after the wedding, and who lived in the same house, hardly ever ate at home. Even animals had names, and his was Bhaskar, but because of his personality everyone called him Rocky.

One day, while Auntie Khushi and I were sitting on the floor, cleaning the home-grown rice, Dev came home and asked her where his new *dulham* (wife) was. She replied by telling him that she was in the shower. He told her to get him some water. She asked if it was to drink, or to wash his hands. It was normal for someone to wash his hands for him – pour water on them while he rubbed them together.

In reply he told her, 'Yes, of course to drink. What do you think, woman? If only I could drown you in it. Shame I can't.'

She went in and got a glass, washed it, returned and started to pour the water out of the clay container. With that he kicked the container, spilling the water everywhere.

'Ah!' gasped Khushi.

'Don't "ah", otherwise you'll get a beating, woman. It takes you a year just to get me a glass of water. You do it deliberately, woman. You're useless, that's why I took another wife. You'd better be careful or you won't get fed or clothed. You'll just rot!'

With that she just replied, 'Yes, of course. Yes, yes…'

'Moti Masi?' I uttered.

'Yes, Sani.'

'Are you all right?'

'Yes, of course I am, dear. I've had a lot worse you know, child, a lot worse. You haven't seen anything yet, child.'

'Really? What's happened?'

'No, child, let's not go there,' she insisted. Then she said, 'You know, children always call me Moti Masi, like you do. When he hears them, he always says, "Yes, call her Moti *Manj*".'

'Doesn't that mean buffalo?'

'Yes, it means fat buffalo.'

'I'm sorry Moti Masi.'

'For what?'

'Because I also call you that, but I think you look cute and cuddly and very warm. I don't say it in a bad way.'

'Don't worry about it, Sania, I don't. But next time, when the neighbour's children come asking for milk or flour or food, and they say "Moti Masi, can we have…", just watch him.'

'Why don't you go to your parents?' I asked. 'Haven't you thought of leaving him? After all, he is only your husband on paper, isn't he?'

'No child, no husband is on paper only. Once married you are married for always to that person, unless of course he throws me out and gives me a divorce himself, which he never will.'

'Why?'

'Because, for a man, it looks good if he has more than one property.'

'Property?' I didn't understand what she meant.

'Yes, property. We mere mortals are property for some men because they believe that a man is wealthy by either his bank balance or by the number of children or wives he has: in return they multiply the amount of children he will have.'

'But he hasn't got any children!' I pointed out.

'Yes, but… well… you're only a child, but you know the saying that a man and a male horse – a stallion – should always be well looked after for they will stay forever young, and so it is seen as the woman's fault it there are no children.'

I could not help laughing at what she had said, and amid giggles I asked, 'Is he?'

'What?'

'A stallion?'

'Oh… a stallion. No, but he does fit into the category.'

'What category?

'The animal category. He's not a stallion, but sure is an animal.'

At this, we both started to laugh. It was surprising that she did not seem upset with him one bit for what he had done. The other two women in the house were out visiting neighbours, and Uncle Anil was out in the field. Moti Masi explained that no one was allowed to take any notice of Dev, as it aggravated him even more, and that this was nothing. But it seemed a big deal to me, especially as I had already experienced something with him myself. I knew what it was like to be intimidated and upset. This culture was alien to me, but these people were real people, with real feelings and emotions. All the same, we *were* worlds apart, but now we lived side by side, through fate of course, not choice.

Dev returned.

'Don't look at me, woman. You will cast a bad omen on me. Keep your eyes down while your husband is in front of you.'

She stopped looking at him for a split second and, once he had moved his feet toward the shower room, she looked at him and shrugged her shoulders.

'Listen, Moti Masi,' I said.

'I can't hear anything.'

'No, listen to him. He's going to sing to my mother outside the shower room and will keep going until he can no longer see her hair. He will follow her to their room, and still sing her songs. Did he do that for you?'

'Yes he did, except the song was different.'

We listened. There was no music, no poetry, just an out-of-tune, croaky voice.

He sang: '*Choo leh neh do nazook honto ko, kuch aur nahin heh, jam heh yeh, kudrat ne joh tum ko bakshah heh, who sub se haseen enaam heh yeh...*'

It meant, *let me caress your delicate lips, God has blessed you with these*, etc.

'You know,' began Moti Masi, 'his favourite singer is Mohammed Rafi, a terrific singer, but he always sang one of his other famous songs to me.'

'Oh yes, which one?'

'Oh, you won't know.'

'Yes I will. Mother listened to them all the time at home. She's very much the Indian woman you know.'

'How does it go?' she thought for a moment. 'I know: *Chaudivee ka chand ho, ya afthab ho, jo bi ho thum khuda ki kasam, la gavab hoh...*'

'I know that very well.'

In tune, we both started to sing it with feeling. I asked her if he was like this, singing her love songs, as well. She replied that all this was an act just to get what he wanted. He played these games with her too, and these games were for, yes, sex – an animal game – for he needed a woman for sex and for slavery. It seemed so true here, but in our house, my home, I had never seen this kind of behaviour, ever.

A few days had gone by and early one morning, as I lay in my bed, I saw him go into the shower room. I knew he was going to have a shower, for he had one every morning, and of course, whenever he did, many times during the day and in the evening, he would always have a towel slung over his shoulder to let the world know that yes, he had had another session and going to cleanse his filthy self again. I quickly got up and ran to Mother. I knew there was no time to lose, so asked her if she had got the money together. She said she had 300 rupees now, and seemed so pleased.

'Only be pleased when you have the passports as well. Have you got them?' I asked.

She explained that she had searched everywhere. There was only one place left and that was padlocked: his chest, the big silver chest that had his things in it. He carried the keys with him all the time. I told her that she would need to get them when he was asleep, and use them when he was in the shower. Then put them back in his pocket before he re-turned, making sure that she had done the deed within that time. She said she didn't have the courage to do this as he would know.

'Well, tough luck, Mother dearest,' I snapped. 'It's a chance you're going to have to take.

She quickly murmured, 'I know.'

'Do it tomorrow, Mama, please, for both our sakes. To-morrow I will come and help you search.'

'But, dear, what if I get caught?'

'We will cross that bridge when we come to it. You have 300 rupees and I will get some too. Maansi and I have already talked to her friend Saiya – the one whose father drives the Suzuki, you know, the Toyota *tucka tucka tuck* noisy, rattling vehicle. He's always going to the market early in the morning to get fruit and vegetables for his father's stall in the bazaar. We will go with him and then from the market we will get the big van, if he can't take us further. We will get a lift to Bombay (Mumbai) or Calcutta (Kolkata), the big cities, and there we can buy our tickets at the airport. I think Calcutta will be better. That's where we flew in to. He can't touch us there. There will be police and security. We'll go, that's it!'

'OK, OK.'

'Tomorrow!'

'Bombay, Calcutta – no. Delhi – yes,' she stated.

'Bombay, Calcutta, Delhi, whatever… tomorrow, yes!'

That day, as always, the evening meal was cooked by Auntie Khushi, Auntie Dina and my mother. Here it was traditional for the daughter-in-laws to cook the meal. If there were no daughter-in-laws, then it would be the mother, but definitely no man would cook. Men living by themselves would normally go to the bazaar and eat at the local hotel, or would eat at a relative's house. On this day, as with other days, we all ate together, huddled up on one bed outside in the courtyard, except for my mother and Dev. They sat near the fire, on the floor. I said to Mother that they should join us. She started to get up, but he pulled her down quickly, and told us that there was no more space on the bed, so they would stay on the floor.

Meals were so basic. Apart from a couple of plates that we shared – Auntie Khushi, Badi Ma and myself – there were three plates for the curry, a flat, woven tray for the chapattis and a couple of glasses of water under the bed. So, as you see, there was no space for two more. Here, people shared plates and glasses, which was just as well because washing-up was a big chore. Sharing plates was also a sign of unity and love.

Water was not available from a tap all the time, so there was a local well where we got water from. Gas was available in a bottle, but was very expensive. Electricity was becoming more and more available, but was always 'on the blink'. Water had to be boiled for washing the dishes, and after scrubbing each thing individually with a cloth and cleansing soap, they were rinsed using only a small amount of water. It was very time consuming; obviously when brains were being handed down to earth by God, I thought to myself, he forgot some parts of the world.

While some women washed up, others tidied, and the rest endeavoured to kill the mosquitoes that pestered everyone at that time of the year. The only time you were safe from them was from November till March, when it wasn't hot, but they say it never really gets cold ever. This was just as well, as what would they do for heating? I know that Badi Ma had told me that when it got cold, she would tuck herself into bed straight after dinner and, if need be, the fire from the cooking was taken in to warm her up, and left in her room for a while. With all these things on my mind, I was, in a way, grateful, but also very scared of the next few days, when I would be far away from all this. Thank the Lord I had met some of these characters as well. The journey had been a real eye-opener for me, and I'm sure for my mother too.

Now that this journey was nearly ending I knew that there were some disturbing things that I would rather forget, but then there had been some that I would never forget. Even on this day, while everyone was busy doing their chores, Uncle Anil was sitting calmly talking to his mother. As for him, my mother's husband, he was busy scratching below and slowly extending his hands to the back as well. How far exactly I could not tell, but then no one dared to keep looking for long. Then his hands would come out and straight onto his moustache, rubbing and winding the hairs together, before moving them around the sides of his nose, with a slight sniff of the aroma on them for good measure. *It's just as well that he didn't touch his head*, I thought as I dozed off to sleep, because his hair was always full of a whole gallon of oil.

The next day arrived.

'Bye, Maansi, and thank you so much for everything. I don't know how I will repay you, but I will contact you once I get back to England.'

'Thank you for taking such a risk for us,' my mother said to Maansi.

We hugged and I kissed her before we drove off with our chauffeur into the dark night. Two hours later we started to see the dawn break, and with it, towns approaching. Soon we saw roads signs for Delhi. I saw the symbol for an aeroplane on one sign, so knew that we could not be so far away from the airport. We were both so scared in this male-dominated world, with their cultural traditions enforced on us – Westerners really – and yet it should have been our second home.

We paid the driver and thanked him profusely for getting us away from danger and into freedom. We both sighed with relief, but knew that we would only feel truly safe when we were on the plane. No one would be able to touch us then. We went to the ticket office and made the enquiries. The next flight to England – London Heathrow – would be in two days' time. That was OK, we both agreed, and asked for a hotel or bed and breakfast. We were told there was some-where just down the road. There were lots of seats available on the plane, so we made two provisional reservations, and could pay and collect our tickets the following day, ready to fly the day after.

We smiled; joy was so evident on our faces. As I looked at Mama, she was happy and laughing aloud. Then, all of a sudden, I could see her face screw up in pain, and full of fright. Her body started trembling. She had seen him, Dev, coming towards us. No words would come out of my mouth. We both ran, but he caught us. We shouted to the security staff. He told them that we were running away because we had all had a domestic argument. He told them to mind their own business and they weren't really bothered anyway. We cried for help but no one took any notice; no one, but no one, listened. Everyone had heard but no one took any notice. Some even laughed at us, but we had nothing to laugh about. Men and women sneered, saying 'foolish women'.

Our journey from the airport back home was intense and full of silent repercussions. We sat separated from one another and didn't dare look at Dev, who was sitting in between us. He was furious and we were gutted.

As we arrived home, I ran inside. 'Moti Masi, help!' I kept repeating this but she didn't come out, and yet I could plainly see her sitting in the room. I ran to her to save us, because I knew we would get beaten badly now.

I opened the door and cried, 'Moti Masi, I've been calling you. Why didn't you come? Oh my God… Moti Masi… who did this? Was it him?'

She sat sobbing, her lips swollen, her eyes blackened and her nose bleeding. It almost looked as if she had had her nose broken by him. Her arms were bleeding too, from where he had grabbed her and her glass bangles had broken. Her hair was a mess; she was unrecognisable, except for her size, but now her face looked a lot fatter because of the swelling. Her breath smelled so I knew that she did not have time to get out of bed. He got her up with his punches. She had remained in that state all that time and all for us; it was my fault really.

'I'm so sorry, Moti Masi, so truly sorry. If I hadn't asked for your help with the money you would not have been in trouble.'

'I thought it would be worth getting hit, so long as it gave you more time to get away. That's why I got beaten up, otherwise I was going to tell him straight away; I thought you both deserved some time to escape. He had no intention of hitting me as he was more anxious about finding you two, rather than dealing with me. But I couldn't think of a better way of buying some time for you, child.'

'Why didn't anyone save you?' I asked.

'He locked the door from the inside. Badi Ma was shouting from the outside. Anil was threatening him, but it was still no use. But child, save her.' Moti Masi looked to where my mother was.

I saw her, how naïve was I? *My own errors of innocence.* I had been so childish.

'Oh my God, Mama!'

She sat silently, looking withered, and very still, tied up in a chain, with nowhere to walk or run away any more.

Tears Behind the Veil

BADI MA, AUNTIE Dina, Auntie Khushi and I all looked at her to make sure she was still alive. She didn't struggle. She sat, chained by her arm to the bed. She could sleep and sit, but hadn't much movement. I went in regularly to feed her and kept telling her how foolish I had been. He could have killed her, but he said he loved her too much. He sang loudly to her like a lovesick Romeo: '*Mujeh ishk heh thuj he seh, mere jaan zindagani, mere paas thera dil heh, mere jaan zindagani,*' telling her how his love for her is his life. If that's how he felt, why didn't he set her free? I felt it was not love he was talking about, but lust.

He never allowed us to talk about anything personal or private, and nor did we dare. By this point we were all so very afraid. He had shown us all what he was capable of. We had to be on our best behaviour and not make matters worse.

Three days had gone by, and when anyone from the neighbourhood came, he quickly got on his feet and told them that she had gone to stay with one of her distant aunties or cousins. They all believed him. Auntie Khushi came that evening and told him that she would take Mama's place and remain captive, if that's what would make him happy. She also told him it was all her plan; she gave us the money and her spare key to the silver chest for the passports and to untie my mother as it was not her fault. He replied by telling her he was not born yesterday but sixty years ago, and therefore was older and wiser than her. Uglier definitely, I thought, but wiser... well, I don't really know!

He told her, blatantly, that she was much too simple and good-natured, hence the reason for her story. The real culprit was that 'bitch of a girl', meaning me. Auntie Khushi then told him that all this stress and depression was bad for any woman who might want to become a mother. A mother. Why does Mama want to become a mother again, I wondered? Auntie Khushi also told him that Mama was looking forward to having his baby, as it would make him very happy, and would complete and fulfil her duty as a wife. He was standing, scratching his head in disbelief. She carried on with her conniving convictions. She told Dev that Mother had missed her period and therefore could already be carrying his child.

'You're not lying are you, woman?' sneered Dev. 'I swear I'll kill you.'

'What's the need? You can kill me anyway.'

He marched up and down the garden in frustration and dilemma, with his hands folded behind his back, looking like a soldier on a mission. He went into the cow shed and came out with a rope. I was sure it was to secure the door more safely, or so I thought.

All of a sudden he came out of his room with the chain that had held Mother to the bed, and flung it on the floor, padlock as well. I quietly walked near Mama's door. She sat there, still silent, her hair was a mess and uncombed, her clothes were three days old, her faced looked tired and sad. I sighed in relief and smiled when I saw her arm free of chains. But that changed quickly as I saw her dainty feet with a rope dangling from her left foot tied to the bed.

I moved closer to her. I was crying now. It was like a scene from the past in the time of slavery, when slaves were captured and tortured by their masters. This was all my doing, not hers. It should have been me in her place. I kept repeating, 'Sorry, Mama. Sorry, please forgive me.'

'Don't be – hush,' Mama uttered quietly. 'I told him it was all my doing and you played no part in it.'

This was the first time in my life that I actually started to hate myself. Our life before was in no way as bad as it was now, and I had made it this way.

'Oi, move, bitch of a girl.' Dev strode into the room. 'She's had a tiring day. Let her sleep now.'

I obeyed straight away. I saw he had a glass of hot milk. He burped loudly and rudely farted. He then passed her the glass of milk, with turmeric (*haldi*) in it, which we all have when our bodies need to recover from pain or injury.

I told Badi Ma that I needed to go for a wee before bed, and before it got really dark. She told me to hurry along. I ran all the way to Maansi's house instead, shouting, 'Maansi, Maansi.'

She came out of the kitchen, shocked to see me. She pulled me inside, as I hurriedly explained to her what had happened to us that day. She said that they had all heard what had happened, as this was a small village where everyone knew everyone else's business. She also told me that the driver had had his leg broken by Dev and his men, just because he dropped us at the airport. Everyone, including his family who relied on his driving to earn money to live, was really worried, as his leg might not mend properly.

She continued by saying that Dev had come roaring to their house, asking where we were, but Beeji told him to go and growl elsewhere as this household knew nothing of it. With that, he left.

'It's just as well that no one suspected you,' I said.

In reply she added that we had to talk silently as even walls had ears. I told her about the punishment that was handed down by His Lordship to my mother. She said that I should convince Beeji to pay her daughter a visit. He would have to release Mother so she could see her guest, her own mother.

With that in mind, I told Beeji that Mama was missing her a lot, was dying to see her, and was not feeling so well. I asked if she could please come and pay her a visit. She agreed. Instantly I felt a burden had been lifted from my shoulders. Would this mean Mama would be released, and for ever? I hoped so.

These last few nights were sleepless and very long. As I reached my bedroom door, Badi Ma smiled at me as if to say 'you're back'. When I passed Mama's room there were voices, almost tender, soft words. Everyone was lying down, so I crept close to their door and put my ear to the hinge.

'Come on now, *mere jaanoo* (my beloved),' Dev was saying.

'No, not tonight.'

'Yes, tonight.'

'No.'

'Yes. Any night and every night. Whenever I say.'

'No, not tied up in this way. Never.'

'You'll still enjoy it, don't worry.'

'Untie me first.'

'Just don't move your foot very far. You can still enjoy it.'

'Stay away.'

'You always say be – what is that word? – romantic.'

'This is not romantic. This is sex and it's sick!'

'Yes, yes, I'm sick for you and you have no choice. So either shut up and let me enjoy myself, or I'll put, or rather tie, a scarf round your mouth. Now, what will it be?'

I could hear rustling and shuffling, but no words. I felt sick. I quickly moved away from the door and cried my sorrows into my pillow. Everyone in the room knew I was crying. No one was able to calm me down. I cried until there was nothing left, no sound, no tears, not even tears of silence.

The next day, everyone was still having breakfast tea when Beeji came in. They all welcomed her, and she asked to see her daughter. Dev quickly said she had gone to her distant aunt's for a visit. Beeji asked who, and where. He replied and she questioned, until she demanded that she see her daughter, and wouldn't leave until she had seen her.

He went in and, after a few minutes, came out, grabbed a jug of water, and went in again. About fifteen minutes later they both came out, him full of pride, her with a fake smile. Mama quickly bent over to touch her mother's feet and Beeji put her hand on her head and offered her blessings. They then hugged. Beeji said, 'You don't look very well.'

'She's had a high temperature for a few days now, that's why,' Dev lied.

'Did I ask you, Dev? I asked my daughter.'

'No, he's right, Mother,' said Mama. 'It's true.'

'I hear you were going to the airport without saying goodbye to me, dear.'

'Well Mother, Dev— I mean, *they* surprised Sania and me by waking us up early that day and taking us to the airport. He booked a flight to the UK for us, mother and daughter, and we didn't even know about it. But then I had a really bad headache and a high fever so he... I mean they, thought it would be better to come back and go another day, when I was better.'

'Is that right, Sania?'

'No, it's not right,' I said. 'We were going to run away. It was all my idea. We hate it here. He caught us at the airport, otherwise we would have been back in the UK. Since then he has had Mama in chains.'

'What nonsense is this? Please go and have a look inside. Where are the chains?' he snorted quickly.

'Look, look, he threw the chain out yesterday. Here... well... it was here last night.' I searched frantically for it. It was gone. 'But anyway, then, since yesterday, he has had her foot tied to the bed with a rope.' I pointed towards Mama's foot. 'See her leg, go on.'

'Show me dear.' There was silence. 'Why, your leg is sore. Is she telling the truth?'

'Ah no, no, not at all. She's joking. He, I mean they, like to play rough – you know what I mean, Mother. I can't explain in front of a child, but we are newly-weds.'

I didn't know whether she was convinced or not, but Beeji shook her head and left in a hurry. I didn't know what to make of it, but I knew Mama had lied to cover for him, otherwise she knew it would get worse for her and for me. I kept quiet.

Later that day I spoke to Auntie Khushi and told her how I feared for Mama's, and my own, life here. She told me that I had to behave and get him to trust us both again, and things would be fine. But for me, things being fine meant going back to England; for her it meant living out the rest of our days with Dev.

'Oh Papa, if only you were alive, life would be worth living again.'

'Don't think like that, dear, for those who die, they never come back. They're in a better place,' cried Moti Masi.

'Moti Masi, what's going to happen to you when he finds out that Mama is not pregnant and you lied?'

'Well, let's not count our chickens before they're hatched.'

These 'chickens' were hurdles that were impossible to jump over, but there was one thing I knew, and that was that I had to behave and gain his trust for both our sakes; after all, Mother had suffered a lot worse than me: a prisoner in her own home. If only he had untied her. That would make things a whole lot better, but she was already trying to side with him by lying to her mother and covering for him.

Thinking about that now, perhaps, as a child, I should not have gone to my grandmother and asked her to come. Then maybe he wouldn't have felt that I was making mischief again. However, more to the point, perhaps I should have not blurted out those words against him to Grandmother. He certainly could not have been happy with me. I know that deep down inside he must have been finding ways of getting back at me.

I felt helpless as there was no one that could help me escape this life. Where could I get advice from? Who would help me? We tried helping ourselves but even that backfired. I felt distraught and helpless, but more so, felt sorry for Mama, as he had her tied to the bed. He knew she could go nowhere and started spending time out in the bazaar, which gave us both a bit of time to talk and bridge the gap that was between us both since the death of my father. As I sat by her side, stroking her hair and tidying it for her, she never once smiled. This was understandable: she was humiliated by what was happening to her.

She said that he had said he was over the moon about her being pregnant. She had been trying to tell him that it was not true, but he would not listen. Being a first-time father at the age of sixty was a dream come true for him. She had told him to untie her if it meant that much to him, but he said when he got the proof, then he would. Naturally I asked her what she was going to do when he found out that they both lied to him. She said she would say she needed to go to the toilet, and then just say she had miscarried. That did seem to be a good plan, but then I asked her how that would be possible. She replied that it would be possible as it does sometimes happen like that. Many times women, especially unmarried women, were given natural remedies to make them lose the foetus. When she has her period, she will say that she has had a miscarriage and he won't know the difference.

In her case, she would just pretend that the clot of blood just came out when she passed urine. He had no experience of it anyway. I questioned her about unmarried girls being pregnant. In our culture it does not happen, surely? She said that normally it didn't, but there were a few cases where girls had gone off the rails.

'Am I off the rails, Mama?'

'What do you mean?'

'Well, that ogre of a man, Rocky, asked if I was new and a virgin.'

'When?'

'Oh, that night when I disturbed you both. The first night I think. What did he mean by "virgin" and "new"?'

'Well…'

'Am I a virgin and new?'

'Well, child, only you'd know but, knowing you, I am sure that you are both of those.'

'What's "new"?'

' "New" means that you have never been with a man, meaning you haven't you-know-what with him.'

'Oh. Thinking about it, I have never even thought about sex or a boy in that sense, and I suppose I am a virgin and new because that's the way I want to stay.'

'Only until you are married though.'

I had no reply. Instead, my face blushed with embarrassment. I had never seen a boy in that way. In my home, I did not have a life where girlfriends and boyfriends existed and anyway, I was a child. When he said that word to me I didn't even know what he meant, but now that I had had it explained to me for the first time, I knew what it meant.

During mealtimes he would take both of their plates inside, and kept reminding her that she was eating for two now. She kept saying to him that if she stayed so stressed she would lose the baby. Even though she didn't really want him to feel guilty, she felt there was no other way but that.

It was the fifth day of seeing her tied to the bed. She walked to the toilet and then screamed from inside as he waited outside the door. She then came out, doubled up in pain, as if it were genuine, and told, or rather announced, that she had lost the baby. He had a very guilty look on his face and she blamed him for the stress and miscarriage. He blamed her, saying she had brought it on herself. He really did look genuinely sad.

I don't know how, but the next day people, especially women, started coming to the house offering sympathy for the lost, unborn baby. Now he told them that because of that, she was not well enough to come and sit outside. That evening she kept asking him to untie her as she had had enough, and then blamed him for her losing the baby, and stressed while shouting that she would not want to have a baby with him ever again. He was raging with anger, then punched her in the stomach and told her how useless she was, as she could not even hold a baby inside. She bent over in pain, as everyone ran to her. Badi Ma said it was awful, as she had only just lost the baby the same day and may never be able to bear him any more children. His nostrils flared in fury.

The following day, before I had got up, he was standing beside my bed. I got a fright as I was the only one in the room. He then bent down towards me and, quietly, spelt out my future to me.

'Now just listen and don't say a word. You are the reason why your mother and I are having problems and lost the baby. The only way that I will free her from that room is when you are married off. So the quicker you marry, the quicker everyone will be happy again. You marry and leave. You and your husband can go to England. I will give you the passport and ticket, and your mother and I will also go to England and settle there. If you don't go then I will have to keep her like that for ever, and the way that she is carrying on, she may die soon. After all, she's not looking good, is she now?'

'No,' I cried indignantly.

'Can you do this one simple thing to save her life or not? Or are you going to be the one who will take her life, your own mother's life? You took your father's life, do you want to take hers as well?'

'No.'

'Good, I'll make the arrangements and let that be our happy secret which we both share.'

'No!'

'No what? It's the difference between saving her and killing her, and of course maybe killing you as well... and anyway, what is the need for you here?'

'What?'

'There is no way out for you otherwise so I think this plan is definitely good for all.'

'No,' I repeated in vain.

'Yes, and remember, if anyone finds out, you've had it.'

'But I'm only thirteen. I'm just a kid.'

'A kid! By the time my first wife was thirteen she had already been married a year. What are you on about? Anyway, you are not a kid, you are a young lady and that is perfect for marriage. This is not a debate. It is either you staying here for ever or you going back to England. Now, what will it be? Listen, you can't go back all by yourself, so why not get married, both of you go to England and then divorce him? You will be set free, but in a dignified and respectful way. You do see what I mean, don't you?'

'Yes.'

'Good. Yes it is then, and let's hear no more.'

'I didn't say yes to marriage,' I stated quickly. I felt like I was being confused and hurried.

'Yes, it is, that's settled. Yes to your freedom, yes to marriage Friday.'

'Friday? But today is Thursday. I can't get married tomorrow,' I murmured.

I would be set free, I thought to myself. *Yes, the only way I would be set free*.

All day I waited for a chance to see my mother, or rather speak to her in confidence and tell her about his plans. Finally I got my chance after the evening meal when the women were doing their chores. Mother was still in her room, but the door was open. She lay there as if she was waiting to rot away, as if she were a very sick or old person with no energy, waiting for death to relieve her of her pains.

He ate with her. He ate a lot and her, very little. He sat on the bed and was talking to her while slowly sipping water. He turned a little to his side and let out a big roaring sound, not from his mouth, but from the other end. And, as a sign of relief he loudly said, 'That's better.' He got off the bed and went off to the toilet to relieve the anxiety that his stomach was feeling. Grabbing this chance, I quickly told Mama of his plan for me. She was shocked, and told me not to go ahead with it, not even for freedom.

Even though she had said no, I could see that the hope held in that word – freedom – meant that she had seen the light at the end of the tunnel. I knew that I had to keep that light on for her and for myself for our journey into the tunnel and out the other end. Without this light I could not think of another way out, or much worse, seeing the darkness for ever; I knew that my mama would not last for very long. Anyway, how could we live a life like this?

That Friday night I was given my wedding attire: a red sari with a few basic trimmings. Lots of young girls had gathered in our house and there was a loud noise of chattering women everywhere. The men were all sitting around, smoking, grunting and occasionally farting. As for the elder women, they burped so loudly that the next village must have been able to hear them. What amazed me was that they all did this with great pride. It was like they were saying,

'We have the money to eat until we are full and so this is the reward, and a thankful message to God as well.' A rug was displayed on the floor and girls sat on it to play the small drum and try to sing in tune. It was not bad really, considering they had hardly seen the world out there.

No one had actually asked me how I felt about this marriage, not even Moti Masi. However, of more important concern to me was the fact that I did not even know who I was getting married to. It had come all of a sudden really. I didn't realise that, without a word, my clothes would be ready and the *uptan* (a blend of turmeric and nutrients) would be applied on my body. This, they say, makes the bride radiant. Henna had been used to decorate my hands, feet, legs and arms, once I had washed off the mixture. I had sat calmly on the rug and accepted everything, all because, for the first time in a long while, I could see my mama sitting freely next to me on the rug; no chain, no rope, just uncertainty!

The next morning I was woken up really early by Badi Ma. She told me to go and bathe before the men awoke, as this was what the bride needed to do. I listened obediently and, as I walked back into my room, everyone was busy, including my mother. Some girls were near my bed with my wedding jewellery. They said they had to get me ready. They called themselves the *Bontiques* but I'm sure that they meant beauticians. Their noses were never clean: how could they know what the role of a beautician was? I got ready with their aid, and then it really hit me – I was getting married. The red veil over my face hid the tears of a child, yet to be broken into a woman. Womanhood was a new part of my life – a life of uncertainty. I cried floods of tears, unstoppable tears: tears behind the veil.

As my tears fell behind the veil, my foundation was smeared and my eye make-up left streaks on my cheeks. No one thought anything of it because in our culture, it is traditional for a bride to cry. My life in someone else's hands. My tears behind the veil. The veil which has now decided this bride's future, the future which will determine this bride's married life, the life of a woman. No longer a carefree teenager, these tears behind the veil are the beginning of my life. These tears moulded the rest of my life. Shouldn't this day have been the happiest of my life? Isn't that how weddings are meant to be – two souls becoming one? Not a beginning of a future life that is already subdued by tears of an innocent child yet to be tainted and marked by a new owner.

Darkness of the Night

'DO YOU ACCEPT this man to be your husband?'

'Yes, I do.'

The music started again. The fire shone brightly and both our scarves were tied to unite us as one. He led and I followed, and we circled seven times around the fire. I could not even see his face, though my veil was thin. At one point, a tear slipped from my eye and onto my cheeks, leaving my eye almost empty for a few seconds. Even then I did not see his face. He was covered in flower garlands that draped over his face.

Everyone ate, except me. Everyone talked and I remained silent. We got up and he sat on a camel. They put me into a *doli* – a bride's travelling box, her companion, which takes her from her parents to her parents-in-law. This small, wooden box held me and a bridesmaid, Maansi, and was carried off, accompanied by the guests, to the new home. You could say it was a chauffeur and limousine all in one: a red box delivering an innocent child to her fate.

I spilled the bowl of rice with my foot, an offering of prosperity, and then dipped my feet into a red liquid. I walked over to the bed, leaving the red traces of my feet on the floor. This was my new bed. This was the bride and groom's bed. The room was full of cheap decorations: plastic fruits hanging from the ceiling, tinsel draping down and cheap glitter on the sheets. And there was a white sheet under the red one. What was that for? I remembered someone saying that the white sheet was the one that protects a bride's innocence. What did that mean?

I sat on the bed and, as I moved slowly on it or when others got off and on it, it creaked badly. Maansi and her siblings sat with me throughout the wedding and here in my new bedroom. I didn't look up at all, as brides are not meant to. It was an excellent way of hiding the tears. I was told not to look up or unveil my face. He – my husband – would be the person to lift my veil and then I would raise my glance up to see him first, and he would see me first as his bride.

The day seemed so long, even though Maansi's mouth didn't stop. She was either constantly talking or eating. She said I was a dark horse and secretive as I had not told her of my marriage. I told her that I had not known myself. She didn't believe me because she was so full of excitement and adventure, dreaming of weird and wonderful things that only happened to married people. But what were these things?

'That's for you to know and for me to guess, Madam Sania,' she said.

'Why is that? I am so upset and have not been able to stop crying, and you, you are supposed to be my friend and yet you are happy.'

'Sania, Madam, all brides cry, well at least all Indian brides. It is the norm, or else they say the bride has no shame!'

'Thank goodness then, that I have shame!' I shouted angrily.

It was getting late and the guests started to leave. Maansi was told to come along and let me rest. It seemed very quiet. I could hear the squeaky noises of the leather sandals on people's feet. I looked towards the door and saw his big feet. He waited so that I would acknowledge his coming into the room. He turned the lamp up a bit, then shut the door behind him. He bolted the latch and sat down, looking straight at me. My veil was still over my eyes but my lips were showing the blood-red lipstick. As he gazed at me, he seemed to turn somewhat human as he said, '*Subhan Allah, kiya khubsorat nazarah heh*,' meaning: 'In the name of the Lord, what a beautiful sight.'

As he said these words I lifted my eyes to look at him when he quickly said, 'Ah ah! Not yet. Not until I unveil you.'

He lifted the red veil from my face and sat mesmerised at what he saw.

'*Yeh gora badam, wah, wah, nasheelah badan.*' (This white body, wow, wow, sexy body.)

As he kept reciting poetic words I knew that he had been watching films and reading a little as well, because he was using words from the Muslim scriptures rather than using Hindi. He was definitely influenced by the inspiring Urdu language, but then, having said that, Hindus and Muslims were all living peacefully as one not that long ago, so I suppose the influence had to be quite real.

I looked up and stared straight into his eyes. I knew that he wanted me to be impressed by him, but somehow I could not find the words to show how unimpressed I was. The only way of explaining what was in front of me was the scene from *Planet of the Apes*. I could have taken any character from that and he would be very similar, so I suppose that was why I could not compliment him at all. But, I had a mission to accomplish, and liking or disliking was definitely not the issue.

His clumpy hands were on my face and neck as he slowly caressed my lips again and again. For a child of thirteen – maybe it was just my age or I was naïve – but this kind of affection did not impress me in the slightest. Maybe if I had had a boyfriend then I would have known what all this was about. I cringed at the feeling of having his spit and saliva on my face, his eyes half closed and his hands going down into my blouse.

'I'm going to be sick. I feel like vomiting. I'm going to the toilet.'

With that I ran and went into a small cubicle near the gate that was the toilet. I stood inside for ages, gasping for breath. I was scared of the unknown. What was going to happen? I had never been here before. I had never even got close to holding a boy's hand before, so how was this meant to make me feel? There were no tears now, but my heart was pounding fast and I knew that I had to control myself and let nature take its course. After all, what choice did I have?

As soon as I got back inside he was standing there in the nude, parading all for me to see. I looked down, full of embarrassment, but then he said quickly, 'Take off your clothes.'

I stood there frozen. There was no way that I was going to do that. Wasn't he supposed to be nice to me? Isn't love meant to be good? Well whatever this was, it definitely was not making me feel good. It was the first time I had seen a man in the nude. It was just as well the lamp did not have a 100-watt bulb in it as it might have cracked the surrounding glass at his sight.

He pulled the draped piece of my bridal sari, tugging at it with all his might. Slowly but surely it started to unwind from my body. All of a sudden I was standing there with only my petticoat and blouse on. He tugged at the shoulder of my blouse as the fragile seam ripped apart. There were fasteners at the back; why was it that he still preferred to strip the blouse off in a very intimidating manner? He began to do adult-like things that I had never even dreamt of, let alone experienced. In next to no time he had forced me onto the bed and he was on top of me. I started to scream in pain and discomfort. He put his hand over my mouth; I no longer had a voice. My eyes showed my awful disgust at what was happening, but there was no one who saw and no one who would hear, as I was silent.

There was no escape from *the darkness of the night*, as the turmoil and treacherous handling of my fragile body continued: tampered with four times at different intervals of the night. As I saw the first flickers of dawn I thanked the Lord that this night had finally come to an end. I could hear the clattering of pots, cups and saucers; breakfast tea was being prepared. Because of my ordeal, and as I was sharing a bed which I was not used to, I had not slept at all. He was sleeping as silent as a lamb. I lay with my back towards him. He was facing the wall and I faced the door. I felt really dirty, and slowly got up and dressed. I opened the door and went into the garden area. An old woman was sitting on the floor next to the fire, making tea. She had blessed me into this house the previous night, so I guessed that she was his mother. She called me to her and told me to sit with her. She asked if I wanted tea, to which I replied yes. She gave me some hot tea. She asked why I had got up so early. I told her that I could not sleep, to which she replied that the first night of marriage, the honeymoon night, the *suhaag* night, was a night of new adventures and naughtiness and, of course, who could sleep on this auspicious night of two bodies becoming one? Sleep would be the furthest thing from a bride and groom's mind.

I tried hard to convince her that that really was not the case, but she only talked, and didn't listen. She then told me to go and have a shower as, before that, people were not allowed to touch anything. In the meantime she would get my clothes and fling them over the shower cubicle. I did as I was told and, after a quick shower, I pulled down the clothes from the wall and dressed.

I went to sit with her again. She started to talk, and introduced herself as his mother. Her name was Suhaani. Her husband was in Germany. She had one son – him, or rather *it* – who had slept all night with me. His name was Suhaan.

Her daughter, Naina, had got married far away and was the one who had looked after the guests the day before at the wedding. No wonder there was hardly any space to swing a mouse in the house; there wasn't a need as there were only two people living here, and I was the third new member. We sat for at least two hours talking about her life: milking the cow or buffalo first, then bringing the milk, making tea and starting the day. She said that her son helped her a lot and Naina would come and help her out now and again.

Soon, women started to arrive, congratulating her for the wedding of her son, and they seemed to be saying secret things to her as well. I thought it was a bit rude. What were the secrets and why in front of me? It was as if they were talking about me. Suddenly, two of them got up and headed off to my room. They came back with the white sheet, which was now stained with blood from the night's activities. They started giggling and shouting, 'He broke a new young thing. She is pure, oh, a pure white thing: a clean undamaged, white, untouched child.'

I knew now what the white sheet was for – proof. If the sheet was not stained they would have given me hell. Suhaani Ma, the mother, told them not to hold the white sheet up. She told them to leave it by the washing and to keep quiet now, as her son was coming out. We all looked at him. He was looking pleased with himself, scratching his head, wondering why he had been woken up.

He headed off to the shower and I went into the room to brush my hair. I put some cream on my face and walked back to the garden. As I approached, the ladies were whispering again, and once again I knew it was about me. We all had tea and rusks, while Suhaani Ma made *parathas* for her son. In the time he had got changed and came to eat. He sat beside his mother like a child, but then he was almost like a child. I did not know his age but he looked about sixteen.

Was this legal? A thirteen-year-old child married to a sixteen-year-old boy?

The day flew by. After breakfast my mother came, along with Moti Masi and Badi Ma. Maansi came with her youngest two siblings and, as they played, Maansi and I talked about the horror of my night. She only laughed and said how romantic it was, how exciting it must have been to live a night of passion, a night of love. For her, a child, it made sense, as everything to her was a game, an adventure. She knew only the innocent things in life, seen through her own, innocent eyes.

Evening had come and we'd just finished eating. The guests had already left as it was beginning to get dark. The ladies who had come first thing in the morning were here again. I knew that something was wrong, but had no idea just how daunting and horrific my next ordeal would be. I was an innocent child, a mere teenager, who knew no conspiracy or cunning thoughts.

The four ladies went into my room. Suhaani Ma was still sitting outside with me. The ladies called me inside. I, like a stupid, naïve girl, went straight in as if someone had offered sweets to a child. My mama had never warned me of strangers and so I listened to them. They asked me to take off my slippers, relax and sit with my feet up on the bed. I did so. They then said that all new brides who are very young need to have this done to make sure that they don't pander sexually to other men. They said I was at the peak of my sexual years.

I listened eagerly but had no clue as to what that meant. They asked me to lie down. I trusted them, so I did. Two of them held my arms and the other two sat on my thighs and quickly lifted up my petticoat onto my face. They pulled down my knickers and put a lump of ice on my private bit. I yelled in horror and pain, because two of them were sitting on me. No one paid any attention – not him, not her. How could they? After a few minutes I could struggle no more. I had no energy left to carry on fighting. They pulled the front area of my private parts and, with sharp scissors, cut it off. They put a wad of old rags on the bleeding area and pulled my knickers back up. They then let go of me. I took the petticoat and put it over my naked legs. My tears were flooding down, but they were silent cries as I knew there was no one any more, anywhere, to hear them. I was numb, so the pain was not so intense. It was more humiliating than anything else. I sat crying and, as the numbness wore off, the pain got worse. I could hardly move I was so sore.

They left and he entered. He asked me what happened. Still crying I told him everything. In response to my heart-wrenching story all he said was, 'Oh well, we can't do anything tonight. You're in pain and bleeding. I'll sleep in Mother's room tonight.'

With that, he shut the door. I felt humiliated to know that only the night before this animal could not get enough of me, and yet today, because I was not in a fit state and needed a shoulder to cry on, he decided to share the warmth of his mother. Is that how animals treat humans? Or is it just male instinct to use women how and when you can and, when she is not usable, ignore her?

I felt like running off to my mama but I was in pain and could not move. I had nothing for the pain either. I lay there until I had dozed off to sleep in my sari. I was still trauma-tised in the morning, but not in so much pain. It was the process of this act that I could not get my head around. I lay there, still, eyes swollen from crying, my voice in a bad way and, emotionally, all alone.

Suhaan entered the room with a cup of tea, put it on the floor, and was heading off when I told him to wait. He stopped and turned to look at me – a child bride, a victim, but his wife. He saw the tears roll down my face and he came and sat by my side. I asked him why he left me the night before. He replied that it was that time of the month for me, so I needed to be left alone. Women are seen as being impure during menstruation. I replied in a hurry that I was not on my period, and neither had I even seen periods as yet; I was not developed as a woman. I explained again to him exactly what those women did. He said that his mother told him that it stops girls from being, 'What's that English word? Yes… saxy. Too much saxy…' and that was why they did this. I asked him why he or his mother didn't tell me or stop the ladies. He replied by saying that he thought whatever they were doing was normal and, anyway, he didn't really know much. That part he certainly got right.

I had not known of anyone who had had this treatment before and so when Mama came at about eleven o'clock to see me, and there were hardly any guests unlike the day before, we had time to talk. She was shocked to hear of my ordeal and said that someone should have told her. She would have put an end to it, but no one would have told her and, anyway, he, her husband, may not have allowed her to interfere.

She told me that it was called a circumcision. Male circumcision was normal for Muslim boys, but never seen in Hindu culture. Female circumcision used to be done in the African world a long, long time go, so she thought, but had not heard of this throughout her lifetime at all. It was not normal practice as far as she was concerned. She was puzzled herself why they did this to me. She said that I must accept this now and get back to normal life as it would help the healing process. But she would ask Suhaani Ma about it. She told me to get up and try to live as normally as possible, but to make sure I didn't hurt that area. It would heal, but when the bleeding stopped I was not to put any clothes over it.

I got up and went for a shower. As I came back to my room I could hear my mama and Suhaani Ma talking about me. I went to get ready. After a while I came out of my room, still walking as if I had a tree trunk between my legs – and not in a ladylike way at all. Here it did not really matter as the ladies walked with their legs very much apart, and sat with a gap of at least eighteen inches in between.

'Where's Mama?' I asked Suhaani Ma.

'Your ma has gone,' she replied.

Naturally I asked her why, as Mama was going to talk to her and, I hoped, would then tell me the reasons for my ordeal. No one had asked on my behalf so I asked myself. She replied that no one had had that treatment done in their family, ever. It was not their decision. She also told me that she had told my mama exactly the same thing. I begged her to tell me whose idea it was. Finally she said she would tell me as I was going to find out anyway. She said that Dev had instructed these ladies, who were so-called midwives or nurses, because Rocky, his nephew, said that I had asked him to provide sexual services, and therefore I was sexually overactive. The treatment was a good way of reducing that.

At the time, I was baffled as to who this Rocky was. She told me it was the man who also lived in the house with Dev. I remembered. He was the one who told me that he could be a man to me. She said she knew nothing of that. I then asked her why she told Suhaan about me being 'saxy'. She said they were Dev's words. She had only repeated them. They were not her words and nor would she use or know words like these. What a shame that, even though we didn't live in the same house any more, he still pulled all the strings. He had promised us freedom, so why this? Maybe that was why Mother had left – to ask him?

I told Suhaani Ma that I would find a way of paying that Rocky back, but she warned me that now I was her daughter-in-law she didn't want me to be involved with the likes of Rocky. She said the less I knew about him the better, for my own health's sake. I insisted on knowing more. She told me that he had ruined many young girls' lives. If I was telling the truth then I had been lucky to have escaped unharmed. Every time his uncle Dev had paid people off and stuck with him, otherwise he would have been in jail by now.

'That means Dev believes Rocky!' I gasped.

'Well, why wouldn't he? As I said, he is his nephew.'

Child Bride, Tearful Cries

A COUPLE OF weeks had gone by and I had recovered physically, but emotionally I was still upset. Suhaan would often laugh and say that, as a child, he always believed that boys had big willies and girls had little ones and now, mine was even smaller. Somehow I couldn't see the funny side of it.

He said that as I was better now he no longer needed to control himself so was going to sleep with me. My mama came nearly every day and said that she had spoken to Dev only once about it and he said that he had to stick with Rocky because no one else did. She said he was unwilling to talk about it and, if she persisted, she would see the back of his hand. At that I did not mention it again either.

This was also another thing: along with the marriage that I, as a female, had to accept as I had no choice, the dominant men made decisions, and helpless women like my mother let them control us totally. In this culture, here in India, is this all a woman's life is worth? Am I a Hindu or a Christian? Well, I am both, so why am I forced into these traditions? Why is it that they say that the man is the head of the family and the wife and children are *his* family? Shouldn't I be a Christian girl living in England? An independent girl? How would I get there? That was still a mission.

'It is so gracious of you, Suhaan, to sleep with me again.'

'Oh, that's OK. I am happy to oblige.'

'I was being sarcastic.'

'And I was being truthful. Nearly two weeks without nookie is no good for a newly-wed boy like me. I've got my reputation to think of. What will I tell my friends?'

'What? Will you tell your friends?'

'Well, yes. Wives and children leave you, parents die before you, but friends stay with you always. There's no better thing than friendship.'

For the first few nights with him, again he persisted on being an animal and treating me roughly as he had done on the first night. I started to bleed once as well. Although it caused me pain and discomfort, he had no real concern. It made me feel like I was there only for the sex and nothing else.

I could say that everything that could go wrong did go wrong, but truthfully it was not the fault of any man as such, even though they played a part. Most of all it was the fault of my own mother. She was an independent-thinking woman, a woman who had her head screwed the right way, so why was it that women wanted to blame men? It is not always someone's fault. Is it that we need to blame someone else, and in this case it was her fault? No one could have taken advantage, could they, really? I suppose there is always the fact that we need to lay the blame on someone else rather than ourselves and sometimes we feel, as women, that we are physically not as strong as men, so deep down inside we feel inferior.

It was now 14 August 1980. Months had flown by – in fact, over twelve – and as I looked at my diary in my handbag, I realised that this day was an important day for me, but had not been recollected. Here, every day seemed the same and I would not know what day or date it was unless I thought long and hard. In England I used to know exactly what date and day it was.

'Mother's birthday,' I said to myself. Turning to Suhaan I said, 'Suhaan, it's my mama's birthday. She's going to be thirty-five today.'

'Oh, how exciting. We never celebrate birthdays here, not really; no parties or going out to eat. We may just cook a cockerel from our courtyard or buy meat from the bazaar and that's it. We don't buy gifts either really.'

'Oh my God,' I responded. 'We used to celebrate everyone's birthday with cards, cake, presents, a party, dinner out – the whole lot. At least, my papa always did.'

'Is that what you want to do for your mother's birthday?'

'Is it possible?' I asked, hopefully.

'If you want it to be. It'll be fun for us all as well.'

'What about money? I don't have any. Well, not much.'

'Don't worry, that's why Father has gone to Germany, so he can earn and send us the money we need. We're not short of money you know. He sends us a lot.'

'Can we buy a card, cake and present?'

'A present, yes. A card – never seen one here, ever. And cake – only in the big bazaar, not here.'

'That will do.' I smiled wholeheartedly as I felt that there was some sort of happiness in my life for the first time in so long. 'Shall we go to the bazaar?'

'Why don't I just go and get what you want.'

'No, no, I have to choose. I am coming.'

'Promise me one thing,' said Suhaan, conceding. 'It is rare for women to go to the bazaar, so keep looking down all the time as many men will be looking at you, as we all do. Ignore them.'

'I promise,' I said and I meant it.

We arrived at the bazaar and walked through, Suhaan pointing out what the small makeshift shops sold. Finally, it had to be a sari as there was no real choice, but that was good enough. We bought a turquoise one, as that had been my papa's favourite colour. We walked on past many glaring eyes. Then I noticed a sign reading STD/PCO.

'What does that mean?' I asked.

'You don't know? It's a phone place.'

'You mean to call anywhere?'

'Yes, anywhere in the world. We phone Father from here.'

'Can I phone someone?'

'Who?' enquired Suhaan.

'Charlie.'

'Who?'

'My friend and neighbour from England.'

'OK.'

We walked up the crooked steps and I sat on the bed while Suhaan told the phone boy that we needed to phone England. He called us into the tiny box room and we picked up the receiver. I dialled the number.

'Hello.'

'Hello. Can I speak to Charlie please?'

'This is Charlie. Oh God, is that Sani?'

'Yes, Charlie! What's wrong with your voice?'

'I was asleep. It's only seven in the morning.'

'Oh yes, silly me, I forgot about the time difference.'

We talked for about ten minutes. I was so happy – almost like the Sania I remembered from back in England. I told her we were both well and would come back soon, but mainly we talked about life and our friends in the UK.

'Bye, Charlie, I'll phone again. By the way, it was so nice talking to you.'

It was so strange. All of a sudden I felt as if happier times had crept up again. I genuinely felt really, really joyous. We walked home together, smiling at one another. Suhaan said that Charlie must have meant a lot to me, as he had never seen me so happy before. He then joked and said that in the future, when I was down, he would get me to phone Charlie.

Lunch was ready and we ate quickly. I put the sari in a plastic bag and we left the house to see Mama. I knew she would be really happy to see me and that she would have forgotten her own birthday this year. It felt really strange going back to the house, Dev's house. Since being married I had not gone there, not even once. Mama came often to see me. She was the only one I needed to see really, apart from Auntie Khushi, who also visited. I was forever to call her Auntie Khushi, as I was no longer a child.

We opened the gate and stood in the courtyard. Auntie Khushi shouted, 'Who is it?'

'Look for yourself!' I laughed.

I ran over to her and she cuddled and kissed me, and told me how much she'd missed me. Badi Ma came out of the room and put her hand on my head and blessed me, while I touched her feet. I sat and talked to both of them, and Suhaan talked quite a lot as well. I then asked where my mother was. Auntie told us that it was Mother's birthday and they had gone to the hotel to have a meal and do a bit of shopping for her as well.

'Moti Masi, we should go now. We have sat nearly all day and she's not back yet. How could she think that I'd forget? But you know, she's forgotten about me. She's never celebrated her birthday before until she's seen me. This year she has forgotten.'

'No, child, sit. I'm sure they'll be back soon.'

'Sania's right, it is getting late. We need to go home,' said Suhaan.

We took our leave with hugs and kisses again. We left the present there. I was very disappointed but didn't want to spoil my own good mood.

On the following day, just before lunch, Mama came to the house, full of apologies. She said she loved the sari and thanked us both. I asked her how she managed to celebrate without me. She did not really. She started to explain how Chaudhrey insisted on celebrating her birthday.

'You mean Papa?' I asked, confused.

'No child, Chaudhrey. Chaudhrey Dev!'

'You used to call Papa Chaudhrey for a laugh.'

'Yes, I know.'

'So why are you calling him the same name?'

'Chaudhrey is just a name given to landowners. Jatts – your papa – I called that because… because it sounded good and—'

'And you call him, Dev, a Chaudhrey because…?' I prompted.

'Because he is a Chaudhrey.'

'And not because you love Dev?'

No answer.

She quickly changed the subject and started to tell Suhaan that on the 23rd it was my fifteenth birthday. They both talked about that, with her promises to celebrate it all together, and make it a big one. Neither of us had remembered our birthdays the previous year.

'Why it is that you called my English father by an Asian name? I hardly heard you call him Thomas or Tom. Why Chaudhrey? Were you ashamed of his name or who he was?

'Of course not,' replied my mother, 'but when I told my family they were disgusted that I was marrying someone out of religion and so I told them that he would change his name and religion, and somehow they didn't seem to be so disgusted any more. I chose Chaudhrey because it is a high-caste name, and a well-respected name as you know now. Most of the well-off men here are given this title – Chaudhrey followed by the first name – and of course you don't necessarily have your father's name here.'

'Forget about that. You should still not call him that name. Just call him Dev!'

With that she just rolled her eyes at me and carried on looking at Suhaan instead.

'Anyway, I think a big celebration is a good idea, Auntie,' said Suhaan. 'You make the arrangements and let me know.'

'All right son, I'll do that.'

She carried on talking to him as I looked on, both comfortable and agreeing with each other.

On the day before my birthday, Suhaan was happy with the arrangements Mother had made. In a way I was also happy. Tomorrow, I was going out of the village into a big town.

My birthday arrived. Outside, a car horn sounded. Suhaan yelled, 'Come on Sani, time to go.'

We both walked together and opened the gate. Next to the footpath was a big van. Inside was my Grandmother Beeji, Uncle Anil and Maansi, Dev's mother Badi Ma, Rocky and Auntie Khushi. Dev was next to the driver and my mother. They opened the door for us and we got in. Mama quickly got out and went into our house. After a short while she came with Suhaani Ma. We three sat together.

The journey was exciting enough as it was the first time we had gone out of our village with permission. There were lots of buildings. I didn't know what area we were in, and I didn't care either. I was just happy being out, almost free, but not quite. There was a very tall building and I knew it was a hotel, and that's where we all got out. The doorman welcomed us in and we all sat at a big table that had been reserved for us.

It was just the right time for lunch – twelve o'clock – and so we ordered to our hearts' content. I even had a coffee, which we didn't have at home. It tasted really good – black and strong, just the way I like it – even though this was not the real stuff but instant. Everyone was sitting, chatting happily to one another. I wanted to avoid all arguments on this day, as it was my birthday so I made sure that I did not sit next to my mother. Who knows, she may have decided just to call him Chaudhrey, and knowing me, it would have got me all heated up. I sat with Auntie Khushi, Maansi and

Suhaan. We talked about birthdays, and how I, or we, the family, always celebrated ours. They hardly ever remembered when their birthdays were and, even if they did, well, most of the time it was an ordinary day. Maybe, if they were lucky, they might get a chicken or rooster cooked and a prayer from the elders.

'Moti Masi, have you never got a present from him?' I asked.

'Well, child, I did one year, when we were newly wed. He surprised me on my birthday and bought a red sari for me, for he said it reminded him of the fact that I was still a newly-wed in his eyes!' she laughed.

We all laughed, especially Moti Masi and me, and even more when she said, 'Romantic, *na*?'

We had all been sitting down for at least three hours, when Mama and Dev said, suddenly, that there was still another treat for all of us, and of course the presents for when we got home. We got back into the van and drove away. I was, once again, just amazed at the quiet scenery – so blissful, calm, very green and beautiful. After driving for about an hour and three-quarters we came to a big, run-down building. We were all told to get out as the van was parked. We went into the building and then realised that it was a cinema, what they called a 'picture house'. Dev and Mama got the tickets for all of us and we sat together in a row. This time I was not lucky, as on one side of me there was Suhaan and on the other side sat Rocky, with Dev next to him.

'I don't want to sit with him, Suhaan,' I said quietly to him.

'Why not? What's wrong with him?'

'I can't say now, but I don't want to sit with him!'

I looked at Rocky, anxious that he might have overheard, and then they looked at each other and started laughing –

laughing at me. I felt embarrassed, so looked straight at the screen rather than at them, and then they stopped laughing. Their joke had worn thin but I was still uncomfortable sitting next to Rocky.

The film started. It was an old classic called *Pakeezah*, starring Meena Kumari. I had already seen it in England, but it was a good film to watch again.

We had been watching the film for about an hour, when suddenly I could feel Rocky's hand on my thigh. I looked at him, but he just ignored me because his actions continued. I tried to take his hand off my leg but he was much stronger than me. I tried scratching his hand, and even though I could tell that I had peeled his skin off, it made absolutely no difference to him. He carried on.

'Suhaan,' I said through gritted teeth.

'Shhh!' was his response. 'Be quiet and watch the film.'

Through the frustration I felt as if sweat was pouring from my private parts, past my thighs and dribbling down my legs. It was a feeling that I had never had before. How could he make me feel so disgusting, and moreover, so wet and clammy?

'Suhaan, I need to go to the toilet.'

'There must be one here in the picture house. Go and ask the staff.'

'Suhaan, come with me?'

'No, no, I can't miss the film.'

'Please.'

'No. When you go at home I don't go with you, do I? Now don't be childish, go on.'

Throughout our whispered conversation he never once looked at me. He was so engrossed with the film, so who was childish?

I got up and left in a hurry. No one from our party looked at me, but others did. I asked a member of staff; the man couldn't help gawping at my breasts all the while I was talking to him. Finally he replied, 'Just in there.'

I turned and sat on top of a hole in the floor, a poor excuse for a toilet, crouched while holding my sari very tightly. I saw a blob, a big droplet of blood trickle into the loo. I couldn't believe it. This was what was making me feel wet. I got up. My pants were full of blood as well. But how could him touching me on my legs cause me to bleed? What could I put there? What could I do? How could I make it stop? What could I wipe myself with? There was only cold water, so I washed myself down, hoping that that really would be the end. I got up, with my knickers sticking uncomfortably to my bum, and clinging very tightly between my legs. There was nothing I could do to relieve this as I had nothing to wrap myself with, and nor was there any toilet paper.

As I came out of the toilet, the door man was standing, smiling, as if he had won a prize. I wondered what he was thinking. I came to my seat but then I felt more blood trickling down. I told, rather than asked, my mother that I needed to go home. Suhaan had said to let him enjoy the film. She couldn't understand my urgency but, because I did not explain but insisted that we leave now, she convinced Dev and the rest followed. Throughout the journey home, which seemed much longer than before, I remained quiet and just stared out of the window. This kept my mind occupied a little, as really I was worried that my sari and the seat I was sitting on would have a patch of red on it.

When we arrived home I said, 'Suhaan, walk right behind me so no one can see my back.'

'Why? What for?'

'Please, just do as I ask.'

He listened and walked behind me. I ran quickly into my room, picked up clean clothes and a couple of towels, and he then escorted me to the shower room. Everyone was concerned about the cake, still uncut, and it was already dark, as well as the presents unopened, and why I had rushed off. The only thing I was concerned with was the 'bloody' issue I had. I rinsed and rinsed but all traces were not eliminated. The water was so cold as I had had no time to warm it on the pot as I normally would have done. When it's hot outside, especially from midday to about four o'clock, it is comfortable enough, and just barely so, to shower with cold water. After all, at that time it is usually around thirty to thirty-five degrees. In the evening, however, even the temperature of the warm day drops, so it felt really cold. I was shaking as I came out of the shower. Everyone told me to come and open the presents. I said I was unwell and going to bed instead. Suhaan looked a little concerned because I was shaking and helped me into bed.

After a little while Mama came in to see if I was feeling any better. I wasn't. She asked what was the matter. I just told her 'nothing' and that I wanted to rest. I could tell in her tone that she was concerned, but I had my own concerns. How could it be that he touched my legs and I started to bleed? How was that possible? Suhaan had also done this, but then his touch was so very different. Was it because Rocky touched me and I did not want to be touched? Is that why? Is that how the body copes?

At that time, still deep in thought, I dozed off, my hair wet and my body aching. When Suhaan came to bed, he told me later, he heard me muttering something in my sleep. He touched my forehead and told me I was very hot. I knew I had a temperature, but my body was freezing. He quickly got a flannel and, after rinsing it in cold water, put it on my head. It felt so unbelievably cold, I threw it off. He gave me some tablets and after about half an hour I started to feel a little better: I was not hallucinating any more.

I did not know what time it was, or where I was, until Suhaan got up. He wanted to be a husband to me, as he used to call it – to have sex. I was tearful as I did not have any energy to fight. He did what he had to and then left me. The only thing I remember was him saying it was good this time as I was 'so hot'. Tears were seeping from the sides of my eyes – *child bride, tearful cries*. I felt that I was drifting away, not into sleep, but slowly into death. Death had called me at an early age. Couldn't it have waited until I was at least my father's age, or even later? I had so much yet to conquer, and anyway, I didn't want to die a child, and definitely not here in India. I wanted to die, not yet, but in the same house, the same room as my father. I wanted to stay and be close to him. *If the only way of being close to my father is death*, I thought, *then let it be, oh God, let it be*, as I missed him so very much.

A Child, Sacrificed

'SANIA, FOR GOODNESS' sake, wake up. Wake up, child. Just look at the state of you. Sania, if not for me, at least for your father's sake, wake up.'

'Papa?'

I knew it was too good to be true. I couldn't die to be with him or live a life, happily, without him. And now she was begging me to wake up for his sake, worse still for his life. *How atrocious*, I thought, but then she had no choice. He was the only way of getting through to me as I really had felt that I was going to drift away slowly, peacefully, in my sleep.

No such luck for a peaceful death or a peaceful life. As I opened my eyes I saw my mother over me; no one else in the room. She started saying how my temperature was sky high, and Suhaan had gone to get her very early in the morning saying that he felt I was not going to make it.

'I thought that too,' I muttered.

'Thought what?'

'Oh, nothing.'

She carried on by saying, 'You will be needing these,' and held out something in her hand. I did not realise what she was talking about. She then asked me if I was listening, to which I nodded. She then held my head close to her and explained to me what they were.

'What are they?' I asked.

'You'll be needing these, dear.'

'For what?'

'For what we all need them for... we ladies.'

'I am not a lady, I'm only a girl. Anyway, did he touch all of you last night so you all started bleeding last night, like me?'

'Stop being so absurd and dramatic.'

'I'm not, really. Seriously, that's why I'm ill. That's why I was going to die of… what is it Suhaan said? Pneumonia. Because he touched me and it upset me so much that I started to bleed. Why and when did he do it to you lot?'

'Who did what? Stop talking rubbish.'

'It's not rubbish, it's true,' I said, exasperatedly.

'Nothing that you're saying makes sense, girl. Nothing has happened except for the fact that you have become a woman of menstruating age and you have started your periods. That's why you are bleeding. But why you didn't tell me, or ask for pads, I'll never know. Now you know, you will get them every month, so always make sure you take Suhaan to the shops and keep them at home so you don't run out, ever.'

She smiled at me. 'More importantly, girl, you have to take precautions now, as you may get pregnant. I don't think you want to become a mum just yet.'

I was still confused. 'I don't know what you are on about. I have heard of periods, but why would I get them when he touched me? And what precautions do I have to take against him?'

'Against who, for God's sake, girl? I mean it; you have started your first period. Now use these pads as you are full of blood. Get cleaned up and use them. It will all be fine. And the precautions are not against Suhaan or anyone; they are for yourself. You take a tablet every day and that will ensure you will not get pregnant. Today, if you are well, I will take you to the lady doctor on top of the hill. She will explain.'

'OK.'

'Listen, Sania, you mustn't tell everyone all your personal details about him touching you. These are personal things between husband and wife.'

'It was not Suhaan, it was Rocky,' I said quickly.

'Don't talk rubbish, child, and don't go round blaming innocent people. Do you hear?'

'I'm telling the truth.'

'Look, I'll pretend you didn't say any of this. I'll wait outside while you get out of your blood-stained clothes and shower. We have already boiled some water, so don't use the cold water. I'm sure you'll feel a whole lot better. Then we will give you some tablets.'

I did as I was told and came back from my shower refreshed, but still had a bit of a temperature. She made me take a couple of paracetamol, which worked pretty fast as I had them on an empty stomach. I then lay outside on a bed and enjoyed the August summer sun in its full glory.

A little later I told Suhaan the whole story that I had told Mama, and what she had said in reply. He said that she was right and I should take her advice.

'What, about my periods or him?'

'About both, as it simply is not the truth about him.'

'How could you doubt me?'

'I'm not doubting you. I think you are just misinterpreting, confused because of your you-know-whats.'

'No, I'm not.'

'You don't know what you are talking about. After all, you didn't even know why you were bleeding, so—'

'So, I don't know what he was trying to do either?'

I went quiet, as I knew that it was a no-win situation. Suhaani Ma and Mama brought the presents from the previous day onto my bed, and the cake as well, which we all ate. I enjoyed unwrapping the gifts. Naturally they were all clothes: saris and *shalwar kameez*. No trainers or jogging bottoms like two years ago, and definitely no football boots like Papa had bought for me. I guess this made Mama happy as her wishes from those years had come true this year. Now I was wearing Indian clothes, eating Indian food all of the time – no more fish and chips – and more importantly, no longer playing football with the boys; just the way she had wanted it to be.

Later on that afternoon Mama came back and took me and Suhaani Ma to the lady doctor. She was told by Dev that Suhaani Ma must accompany us, or another adult, as proof of where we were going. She did as she was told. He even booked a van to drive us there. The driver was someone he knew and was given instructions not to let us out of his sight. The drive was only a couple of minutes and, as we waited to see the lady doctor, there were many other women waiting also. Mama asked Suhaani Ma if she needed any medicine for her asthma. She said she didn't.

When it was our turn, Mama said to Suhaani Ma that she didn't have to come in if she didn't want to, as she didn't really need to see the doctor. Suhaani Ma agreed, and Mother and I went in. The doctor was briefed by Mama, and then she showed me different things that would and could prevent me from getting pregnant: contraception and birth control she called it. Whatever, it made no sense to me as it was all so new. I decided on the tablets as I thought that I could remember to take these.

The doctor then asked Mama how she was feeling now. I asked her straight away, 'When were you unwell?'

'I'll explain later,' she replied.

As we left the surgery with Suhaani Ma, Mama shook her head to let me know that I shouldn't ask her now, so I didn't. We went back to our house and Suhaani Ma started to do her normal chores. Mama took this opportunity to explain to me what the doctor meant. She had become pregnant but knew that she did not want to keep the baby because, firstly, she had a married daughter who could be a mother soon herself, and secondly this would be another hurdle for her to jump as another passport would have to be made to take the baby back to England with her. Also, she thought that maybe he would not allow her to take the baby back. Who knew how it would turn out?

I had heard the word 'passport' again, and quite frankly I had not registered the other details so well.

'So, where are the passports?'

'I still don't know. I have looked in the old place but they are not there. I have looked everywhere in our room, and the main room, but have not found them.'

'You have to try harder.'

'I know, child. Anyway, I pretended I had women problems and told Dev to take me to the lady doctor. Then I told him to wait in the reception as it was a female matter. I told the doctor that I needed an abortion. She told me that if I was absolutely sure then she could arrange a day and time for me to come in and it could be done. I told Dev that I had problems with my insides and that she would correct them. He believed me, and so I had the baby aborted. He did not suspect a thing.'

'And the passports?'

'Have you actually listened to anything I have said?'

'Yes, I did actually. You said you have not found them yet!'

'And?'

'And that means you're not trying hard enough.'

She looked at me in a sorrowful way while nodding her head, then left. My dreams were being dreamt once more. That evening I told Suhaan that I wanted to go back to England and he could accompany me, but only if he wanted to. His reply was not what I had expected. If you mention

England to anyone there, they all jump as fast as they possibly can. Instead he said, 'I am sorry but that is not possible because, until my dad comes back, I have promised him never to leave Mother by herself, and she will never leave her home.'

I then suggested that I go and he could come after I sent sponsorship forms to him once his father came home. He replied that a wife's place is with her husband, and so I could only leave with him, and at the moment no one knew when that might be.

'Oh God, why does this keep happening to me? I never wanted to come to India. I never wanted Mother to marry and I definitely didn't want myself to be married. The only thing I want, and have wanted since I got here, was to go back home to England. Why can't I go, Suhaan? Why not? Please, if you love me, you can't refuse, please.'

'Love? I only love my mother and father, for you know what they say – wives will come and go but your blood, your own flesh and blood, your parents, never desert you. You can't replace them. You can marry many times but you can't get another mother. Anyway, I have never said that to you, have I?'

'No, you haven't, but I assumed—'

'Stop shouting both of you,' Suhaani Ma yelled.

I turned to her. 'Suhaani Ma, please, I want to go back home. Please, please…'

'I'm sorry, child, but he is right.'

'If you don't let me go, then I'll run away.'

'If you do that, and you can try, believe me, I'll have you shot,' growled Suhaan.

With that I became silent as I saw the anger on his face, and a gleam in his eyes that looked like pride. He then said that a wife and daughter-in-law should be the pride of the family, and respected, but if she does anything disrespectful then she would need to pay, whether with a punishment or with her life.

With this thought in mind I sunk back into depression. I saw that I was as much a slave and prisoner here as I was in Mother's house. He, Dev, had promised me freedom. I told Mother to remind him of his promise, to which she replied, 'Well, he has done what he had to and now it is up to Suhaan.' As far as Dev was concerned he did not have anything of mine.

There seemed absolutely no way out once again. Why did I marry? Was it just to get her freed? These awful, depressive thoughts ran through my mind. The coming of winter didn't help as it had started to get colder in the mornings and evenings. There weren't many cloudy days, but I felt as if the dark greyness of the clouds was inside me. Diwali had come and gone, as had *Karvachoth* – a fasting for the husband – which I had not kept, and other festivals and festivities arrived, but I had not noticed or enjoyed any of them.

Since the argument about wanting to leave, mine and Suhaan's attitude and tone towards each other had changed completely. We never spoke nicely to each other. It was as if we had created a big rift between us. Up until this point the only closeness we had was for the sake of sex, and even then it was one-sided; I simply just put up with it. We had lost this as well now. He was, at times, aggressive when he wanted sex; he would just grab me whenever he wanted.

Mother had accepted the idea that she and I were here for ever. Spring showed its colours again and the warmth of the sun shone more brightly and for longer. Spring gave way to summer and once again we were approaching Mother's birthday. She had not become pregnant again, as far as I knew. As for me, I had, like a good girl, taken my Smarties every day as prescribed by the good lady doctor to keep me well and in the best of health. I told Suhaan that, considering I had lost all that blood, I had become anaemic and so these tablets were vitamins and iron. He was young and naïve so believed me.

Suhaan would often say how we were going to have lots and lots of children to fill up the house, and how the laughter would fill up the emptiness in our family. My emptiness could never be filled. It was because of the absence of my father, and there was no way I wanted to become a mother while I was so young. I had never known of these tablets, or 'Miracle Smarties' as I called them, before. I had absolutely no knowledge of such things, but luckily for me I was made aware of them. Suhaani Ma would often say how she was looking forward to the sound of small feet in her household, and would ask politely why I was not pregnant yet. I always replied that I didn't know. She would then ask if everything was OK and, 'I do hope you're not controlling nature?' To this I always replied, 'No, of course not.'

I knew she was also asking Suhaan about this as I had often heard her enquire, 'You are both OK together, as husband and wife, aren't you, son? You know what I mean, don't you?'

He would always nod his head, with his eyes lowered, and say, 'Of course, Ma.'

Since the passport incident I knew why Suhaan and, to some extent, Suhaani Ma, were not as close to me as they had been. I knew their reasons, but why my mother visited a lot less and kept herself at a distance these past three months was a puzzle to me. The only people still close to me were, of course, Maansi and Auntie Khushi.

The night before my mother's birthday, 13 August 1981, I felt I needed to look and appear happy again for her sake. I talked to Suhaan and his mother about taking Mama and her family out, like we did for my birthday the year before. They said that would be a lovely idea as they had never taken anyone out, ever. Suhaan and I would go after breakfast and tell Mama of our plan for her birthday. If she had anything else planned, well, she would have to cancel, and that was that!

I put on my red sari and brushed my hair straight so it reached my bare waist. I walked with Suhaan, who looked quite dashing in his *kurta* and *shalwar*, with a hint of golden embroidery. We shut our gate and, slowly so as to surprise them, opened theirs. Their home seemed very bare. Badi Ma and Auntie Khushi sat on the bed sipping breakfast tea. There was no sign of anyone else at home.

'Where is everyone else, Badi Ma?' I asked.

'Well, well, well, they've gone out.'

'Oh no, I had a terrible feeling that they might leave early to celebrate Mother's birthday. Oh, if only I had thought of it sooner. Like last year they've gone out again without me. She promised she would remember me this time. After all, who else does she have?'

'Oh well, never mind, Sania,' said Suhaan. 'We'll just wait. Maybe they might come back after lunch? Otherwise we can go out in the evening instead.'

'Oh shut up, Suhaan!' I yelled.

'For once this child has the right to be hurt and angry,' began Auntie Khushi. 'Radika and Dev have both gone to England early this morning. I'm sorry, child, really Sania, I'm sorry.'

Auntie Khushi looked genuinely as shocked as I was. My own mother had sacrificed my happiness for her own. *A child, sacrificed. That was me.*

Blood, Sweat and Tears

WE OPENED OUR gate with our heads bowed down: me, because I felt shame and betrayal due to my mother; Suhaan, because he could see how hurt and sad I was feeling. There were no words that could describe my feeling of being let down, abandoned – by my own mother. He knew just how upset I was. Auntie Khushi had said she only knew early that morning, and was not told about it beforehand as she may have told me; that could have so easily have been true. It was so clear that I was upset, but for me the biggest worry was who would I get my passport from? He, Dev, had it. Where was it now and how could I get a new one? Suhaan was not willing to help at all. He played the game of ignorance so very well, whether deliberately or not.

I sometimes feel that ignorance is a sweet antidote to reality. Rather than facing the bitter truth, it is better to be ignorant of it, or at least that's what Suhaan always led me to believe. The night of passion, for Suhaan anyway, which could have been, did not happen. The night was to be a very long and tearful one for me. I spent it crying and reflecting on the past year and a half of being there. Before, at least there were two passengers on this torturous journey, but now my only companion had left me for another in the hope of making her life bearable again. Little did she know, or maybe she did, that the girl she left behind she had left to rot away. How could a mother remove a limb of her own and leave it behind?

I kept saying to Suhaan that I needed to have my passport back, as I would need to go back to England one day. He too would be eligible to accompany me. I emphasised how urgent it was that I find out what Dev had done with it. Suhaan just replied that it was not necessary as yet to get it, or find out its whereabouts, as we were not going anywhere in a hurry; we could get another when needed. No matter how many times I cried, aloud or in silence, he never calmed me down or showed any feelings of sympathy. Why was it that he did not show me any compassion like I remembered Papa showing Mama? Real feelings were alien to my husband as there was no tenderness, respect or understanding. This was a life that I could never have chosen and endured for myself, but it had already happened.

After breakfast tea I told Suhaan that I needed to phone home, in England, and find out about Mama. It would be morning there now and she would be getting up for her bathing and prayers. Suhaan said we would phone at lunchtime, and by that time everyone would be up. I accepted this as it did make more sense. I kept looking at my watch, counting the hours – four hours forward for India and four hours back for England – but it didn't make time move any faster. Auntie Khushi came and wrapped her big, fleshy arms around me. This soothed me: she was like a mother figure, comforting and sharing my pain.

There wasn't much that I wanted to say to her today and she didn't talk very much either. For me it was as if there had been a death in my family. There was a sombre mood reflecting my grief. Twelve o'clock arrived and I rushed off to tell Suhaan. He was already waiting for me, knowing how eager I was. We walked in silence. I behaved myself without being reminded, keeping my head covered and down while moving through the bazaar.

We reached the telephone office and Suhaan gave them the number to call.

'I'm sorry but there's no reply from this number, Suhaan.'

'No, Suhaan,' I interjected. 'Let it ring for longer. Mama has to pick it up. She can't ignore me.'

'Please keep trying again and again,' Suhaan asked.

'No problem,' replied the telephonist. He kept trying and trying but it was of no use.

'Shall we go, Sania?'

'No. Try Charlie's number. Maybe she's gone next door.'

'Oye.' Suhaan told the telephonist once more, 'Try the other number.'

'OK.' This time someone did answer.

'Hello Charlie, it's Sani. How are you?'

'Hi, Sani. Nice to hear from you, and yes I'm well. And you?'

'I'm fine.'

'How fine are you? As fine as that day when I asked you?'

'Well, that day my papa had died.'

'And today, you sound the same.'

I burst into tears. She pleaded with me to tell her but only sobbing came out. On the other end of the line there was no voice, but just more sobbing. I stopped crying and then she asked more about what had happened.

'Please Sani, tell me what's up?'

'Mama has left me here and gone.'

'Gone where?'

'She didn't tell me, but back to the UK.'

'Really?'

'Charlie, please go and knock and tell her to come to the phone. Use you key if you have to, and tell her it's urgent.'

'OK, I'll go now. I'll hurry, don't worry. I'll get her for you.'

With that she put her receiver down. Three minutes had gone by and then, suddenly, someone picked up the phone.

'Mama, Mama, is it you? Please speak.'

'I'm sorry, Sani, it's only me, Charlie. I'm so sorry that there is no one there. The house is empty and no one has been there either. Your mother has not come back to her house.'

'Are you sure? Did you check?'

'Yes, of course, Sani. Give me your number and as soon as she comes or I hear from her I'll be sure to phone you straight away, I promise.'

'I know you would, Charlie.'

We carried on talking for a while. I talked and she listened and sympathised. I told her everything, but of course in English. She was shocked as to why my mother had done this. She couldn't understand.

I finally put the receiver down, still feeling disillusioned. My mother hadn't just cut me out of her life, she'd cut the blood tie of the umbilical cord to create a vast distance between us – a distance between two worlds on the opposite sides of the earth. I had to accept this as I knew that Charlie was not going to know any more than me. Mama had made a new life for herself with Dev and I was not part of it.

The following day I thought I had better give it one more try, and so I wrote a letter and asked Suhaan to post it. But then I changed my mind. I wanted to post it myself to make sure. I sent one by ordinary mail, and another by registered post. This I insisted on because it was the only way of making sure that the letter would actually get to the right address. A week later the telephone man sent a young boy to come and tell Suhaan that Charlie from England had phoned for me. I was full of excitement. If Charlie had phoned that meant that there must be news of Mama. I got ready quickly and we left. We did not wait for her to ring back: we phoned ourselves.

'Hello, Charlie. Where's Mama?'

'Hello, Sani. I'm sorry but there is no news about her. I only phoned because I found your letter you sent for her, and so I thought I'd let you know it had arrived, but your mother hasn't.'

'What?'

'I'm really, really sorry Sani. I wish there were something I could do for you.'

'There's nothing that anyone can do for me, Charlie.'

These were the last words I said to Charlie. A week later the registered letter had come back. No one opened the door to sign for it so it was returned to sender. No one wanted my letter. If she did want it she would find it on the side table near the front door, right next to the telephone, in our house back home in England. She couldn't miss it if she tried, so Charlie had told me a month later when she had phoned again, although it seemed much longer as time was really beginning to drag now. This time my hopes were not high at all. She told me that she would leave the letter there, just in case; after all, Mother would have to come back. Where else would she go? I had run out of ideas and knew of nothing that I could possibly do to help myself. I began to accept that this was my life for ever now. A life without my mama and my papa.

With Mama out of my life I began to spend more time with Maansi. Suhaan did not mind as he knew that I was going nowhere. She had no idea either as to what I could do, even though her brain was always working overtime. As Mother and Dev were no longer living here, their house would often be empty, especially when there was a death in the village. Everyone went, except the children, and it was on one of these occasions that Maansi and I, with her siblings, went out into the fields to roam around freely.

It was a crisp November morning and the announcement of an old lady's death meant that everyone had gone. Maansi and I had gone into the fields, and this time left the little ones at home where they would be quite safe. We were sitting on a big tree branch, talking about life in England. We then talked about the incident in the cinema and my periods. She did not know what to make of the story of Rocky touching my leg; it all seemed quite exciting to her. She was laughing loudly when, suddenly, we heard a man's voice.

'Oi! What are you both laughing about so loudly?'

We looked around. It was Rocky. We became silent. What a coincidence that we were talking about him and there he was. It is said that if someone turns up like that, while being talked about, it means that they will have a long life. I was, of course, hoping that that myth would not come true for him. He stood looking at both of us, and turned to talk to me.

'Listen, I need to talk to you.'

'Well, I don't want to talk to you,' I replied indignantly.

'I've got something to tell you.'

'There's nothing that you have to say that I want to listen to.'

'You will, when you know what I know.'

'Get lost and leave us alone, or else,' shouted Maansi.

'Or else what?' said Rocky.

'Or else… or else… we'll scream,' she replied nervously.

He just laughed in her face. 'It's about England.'

'What? My passport, or my mama?' I asked.

'Meet me here tomorrow at the same time to find out, or else you'll be the loser.'

'Loser?'

'Well, yes, if you don't meet me, you'll never know what I have to tell you. You'll never know, will you? And listen, don't bring her along with you,' he said, pointing at Maansi.

'She'll be here,' said Maansi. 'Don't worry. But just make sure that the information is good or—'

'Or else what? You're going to get your mother on to me? Ha, ha, ha.' He laughed loudly, ridiculing her.

She looked embarrassed and he looked proud. She looked away from him towards me. He arched his broad shoulders and started to walk off, singing an Indian movie song.

'Anyway, where were we?' I said.

'Forget that, Sania Madam, make sure you get the passport and everything from him.'

'If he even has it. And what's the "everything"?'

'Everything you need to know, like where they've gone to. He must know where his uncle Dev is. That way you'll know when and how to contact your mother.'

'Yes, you are so right. He must know that at least.'

Soon we could see a few people coming down the path, which meant that the funeral was over and people were returning back home. A lot of them prayed as they passed the graveyard and asked the good Lord to bless all those who were buried there. Maansi said it was time for her to get back home; she had to see her younger two and get the tea on as well. We both made our way home and waved to each other as we went our separate ways.

Once back at the house, Suhaan asked, 'Where have you been all this time?'

'Oh. Just with Maansi, in the graveyard.'

'All right.'

I smiled at him, but he was too busy to notice that. He was busy feeding his dog. That night I kept thinking and planning in my head exactly what questions I was going to ask Rocky, and what my responses would be to some of his explanations. The more I thought, the more my head became muddled. Finally, I decided on just asking about my passport and Mama's address. The longer I stayed with him the greater the chance I had of being caught with him. If I ever got caught everyone would say that we were doing something wrong, for sure.

The next day I kept looking at my watch waiting for the time to come around.

'I'm just going out to meet Maansi and I'll be back soon,' I said to Suhaan.

'You met her only yesterday!'

'I know, but she's the only friend I have. Please can I go?'

'Let her go, Suhaan,' said his mother.

With that, he nodded his head. He could not refuse his own mother. I walked over to the fields, making sure that no one was following me. I waited but he was not there. Suddenly someone put their hand over my mouth and dragged me into the animal barn close to the tree we had sat on the day before. It was full of hay. In an instant I was thrown down onto the floor. It was Rocky.

'Why did you do that?'

'Shut up or else people will hear us.'

'All right. What information do you have?'

'What information?'

'Yes, that's what I said, what information?'

'Well, let's see… What's it worth?'

'I don't have any money so can't offer you anything.'

'You must have something I want.'

'No, I don't, no money… Oh yes, I have my jewellery and watch.'

'I don't want those. I want to be paid in kind.'

'What? What does that mean?'

'It's OK, I'll show you.'

He shut the barn door behind him slowly. It became quite dark as there were only wooden windows that let in a limited amount of light. He threw himself down on top of me. I tried to get away but he was much too strong for me. His grubby hands were on me, his moustache tickling my face. His lips were pressing against mine so tight I found it impossible to breathe. I kicked out as much as I could but it was no good. I was trying to shout but little noise came out of my mouth, but my silent tears could not be stopped. As my tears ran into his mouth he stopped.

'I'm on, please stop,' I said hastily.

'On what?'

'On my you-know-what... what ladies have.'

'What? I'm not a lady, so I don't know.'

'Please, I'm on my period, so I am bleeding a lot. You can't do this when I'm on.'

'What rubbish is that?'

With those words he continued his rebellious actions as I lay there crying in disgust. My blood, his sweat, my tears, on me. He was very active and the sweat from his forehead dripped onto my face. My tears in his mouth, not that that deterred him, nor did my blood make him stop.

Blood, sweat and tears.

'Quickly tidy yourself up and wait a little while after I leave, then you go.'

'What about the information?' I asked through my sobs.

'We'll see about that another day.'

With that, he left. I lay there, on the straw, feeling disgusted, ashamed and so very dirty. Why did I feel so dirty? It was not my doing or my sin. And anyway, had I not had sex before? Yes, I had, but the reality of it was that I had never been raped before. I had never heard of being raped, except for what I had read in books. From that I had pictured, in my mind, a scene of what rape would be. I wondered if being sexually abused and rape were the same thing or different. I had been forced into having sex but then wasn't that the same as what Suhaan had done?

Suhaan forced himself, as did Rocky, but at this particular time of the month Suhaan would be lenient. As far as Rocky was concerned it made no difference to him at all. I thought to myself, how come I felt so bloody dirty and he had accepted it as normal? Is it normal to feel the way I was feeling? Is it normal for him not to mind? Looking back on it, it was almost like a situation where two lovers had sneaked away from home to be together, not out of love, but because of lust. But that wasn't how it was and I did not want it to happen again.

The sad fact was that I had come willingly to seek information, and instead had been subjected to the brutal, vicious, sexually hungry animal that he was – this dog lusting for his own pleasure. In this society men and women find an excuse for their actions by saying that, 'men are dogs': they can stray at any time and once off the lead they can do animal things to fulfil their desires. This is not really the truth. It is just a poor excuse; a poor excuse for men but a reality check for women as they are left with the emotional scars from their ordeals, whether it be abuse or rape. The fact is that I had said no. I did not give him permission or lead him on, but I had to face the traumatic repercussions of that awful day. He did not.

Lust and Regret

A QUICK ROMP in the hay – that's what everyone would have said, were I to tell. That's what Maansi said. Who could I tell and would anyone actually believe me? They would have doubted me, even though they didn't really know Rocky. Or was it that they would prefer to remain ignorant? Suhaan hadn't believed the cinema incident, so why should he believe this? I knew he would not and I was scared of being labelled as unfaithful by my family. I could not take the risk of them doubting me for the rest of my life. Also, my main concern was still them letting me go back to England – this could remain just a dream rather than becoming a reality.

I knew one thing for sure: people would believe him and not me. I did, however, have to share my story with Maansi as she asked me about my meeting with Rocky. I could not lie to her and so told her the truth. She kept asking what was it like – was it exciting? She didn't once say, 'Oh God, how awful,' but instead, 'Was it all romantic? Fancy that.' She didn't understand the seriousness of it, being a teenager. But then, so was I. She didn't see it as a big thing, but just understood it as being something that happens!

As I looked glum and upset, she all the while smiled and giggled as we talked about it. All the talking in the world, and the reflection of that day, lived freshly in my mind. Little did I know that that one mistake made by someone else was going to mean that I would have to pay for it so very dearly, as I later lived to regret.

December arrived and it had got a little colder. I was not feeling very well. I knew it was the cold weather that was making me ill. There was no heating in the house, hardly any warm water and no parental love to keep me warm either. I phoned Charlie a few times, and also tried my own house, but no one replied. Charlie reassured me that no one had gone to my house, not even Mama. What I could not understand was where she had gone. That was the only home she had in England. Where would they be living? Why hadn't she written or phoned me? Didn't she know that she was the only family I had? How could she turn her back on me?

I didn't know where to write or call and, really, I was at a dead end. I was feeling unwell, both physically and emotionally, in my mind and heart. My vomiting was not stopping and I tried to hide it from Suhaani Ma because I did not want to tell her what was upsetting me. By January I was still not better and how could I be? The coldness had not ended in the mornings and evenings. One day I was feeling so cold, miserable and so very lonely, and needed a big hug, so I went off to see Auntie Khushi. She did what she always did best – kissed and cuddled me, more than my own mother did. The tighter her hold on me, the more emotional I started to get. The longer her clinch, the more tears started to run down my cheeks. The more she patted and rubbed my back, the louder my sobbing became.

'What's the matter, child?' she asked.

'Moti Masi, Moti Masi, I miss Mama so very much.'

'I know you do, child, but you can't upset yourself like this.'

'Why not? What do I have to live for? I wish I could kill myself.'

'Please child, don't say or even think it. It is a sin!'

'Sin? I haven't committed any.'

'Why, child, I never suggested that you had, but why are you so touchy today? Has someone upset you or said anything to you? You can tell me, you know that, especially as your mother is not here.'

'I know but, but—'

'But what? Spit it out child. It's not good to have secrets, especially those that are a burden on our minds.'

'No... Nothing, really—'

'No, nothing really but...? But what, Sania?'

'Well... well...'

I told her. I told her everything.

'Are you telling me the truth, child?' she asked.

'Are you doubting me?'

'No, of course not, but child, why didn't you tell me, or anyone, before today?'

'I did. I told Maansi.'

'No, I mean an adult.'

'So? What can you do? Nothing, that's what. What's the point of telling anyone?'

'Don't worry, child, I will ask him...'

'OK.'

'Why aren't you well?' she asked. 'What's the matter? You're looking pale.'

'Well, I feel cold most of the time, I don't want to get out of bed, I'm tired all the time and I'm vomiting as well. I've caught a bad chill.'

'Vomiting?' Auntie Khushi looked at me gravely. 'Have you had your period this month?'

'No, I... We... Thinking about it, I haven't had one for two months now, but anyway, what does that have to do with my not feeling well?'

'Oh God, child, everything. You are pregnant. You're going to be a mother, oh Lord! Why doesn't he punish the culprits rather than the innocent?'

I sat silently, crying now, as I took in all the information she had given me. Me, a mother, a mother at sixteen! Oh God, I should have been doing my exams and thinking of college and university. I wanted to be a doctor like my father, not a victim or a patient like I was now.

'You know, child, you can't be sure who the father of your child is, can you? It could be either of them. Do you want me to talk to Rocky and do you want me to tell him about you being pregnant?'

'Well, how can I be sure? I don't know, do I?'

'It is more than likely that you are pregnant with his child, or rather that he has fathered your child. In that case he should know about it, but it could make problems for you as well. He may want a test done or may want the baby. How will that affect your marriage? Everyone will know and hear about it. And then there's the other thing of... well, people may never believe that you were forced. They may think that you had an affair. Are you listening, child?'

'Yes, of course I am. But I don't want to keep this child. Mama never kept hers and I can't afford to have more problems. After all, if Suhaan found out he might throw me out. Where would I live? Besides, why should I have a baby forced upon me, especially as it is Rocky's and not Suhaan's?'

'Don't do anything hastily, child.'

'It's not through haste, it's reality, and I don't need to think about it at all. I will go and see the lady doctor, the one who gave me the pills, and get it sorted like Mama did.'

I left quickly. Auntie Khushi was calling after me. When I got home Suhaan could tell that I had been crying and asked what was wrong. I didn't tell him, for the obvious reasons, and just replied, 'Nothing.'

The next day, Auntie Khushi came and told me that she had spoken to Rocky about it that day. She said that he denied it all, saying that he was in the bazaar, and she could ask his friends. With that tone and reply of his, she said she did not mention the pregnancy at all. She asked if there was anything else she could do for me. I said there wasn't, as I really had to solve this one myself. For the first time in my life this problem, and my situation, was directly linked to other people's respect for me, and I could not take a risk with it. That's the way I had been brought up and wanted to remain.

Deep down inside I desperately needed to talk to my mama but that was not possible, in spite of the fact that I had phoned so many times. There was always no answer. Charlie had not seen or heard from her either. During the winter days Suhaan would often go to the bazaar for his afternoon tea with the local men. This was when Maansi and I could spend time together.

One day, an ordinary day, Maansi and I were on the tree trunk again talking about my decision and how I came to that conclusion. All of a sudden we heard soft footsteps. We both quietened down and looked around. It was him. *Oh no, not again*, I thought. But it was.

We looked stunned to see him. We were silent. Suddenly he spoke, saying that he had heard that I had been phoning my mother but had had no luck in contacting her. Maansi quickly replied, 'Yes, so what? What's it to do with you anyway? So, get lost.'

'Huh, little girls playing with dolls still. Anyway, I wasn't talking to you.' He turned to me. 'Oi, you, you won't find her cause she is no more.'

'No more what? No more means death. She's not, she can't be, can she?'

'Ha, ha! I'm afraid to tell you but you'll never see her again.'

'Is she dead?'

'You figure it out yourself. You're a married girl now. Grow up and try and understand adult stuff. If she was still around why hasn't she contacted you? Where can she disappear to?'

'Why are you playing mind games with me? Tell me the truth. If you know it, don't play games with my head!'

Maansi and I then ran quickly to Auntie Khushi and told her. She said that they had not heard from Dev or Radika since they left, as far as she knew, but what the truth was, was hard to say. She also said, 'Why would he say it unless it were true?' But he was capable of anything, so who knew what was going on in his mind.

The next day she said that Rocky had told her that it was very strange, he felt, for them to disappear into thin air, so they could be dead. Who could know? This may be especially true for Radika as she would never disown her own daughter. No one made this day one of mourning, as no one knew of their whereabouts. They thought nothing of it. As for me, however, I could not believe it, or rather did not want to believe it. Deep down inside it was troubling me, but there was nothing I could do. It was on my mind all the time. And it was her fault – my mother's fault!

With this news on my mind I had not left the house in days. Maansi came after a week and said that she felt that I might be feeling better now. I wasn't really. I was just scared of the unknown. The sickness had worn off but my mind was occupied all the time with thoughts of what could have happened to them. Suhaani Ma would often sit and dwell on what really could have happened, but a humble woman cannot do much but just think.

As for Suhaan, he said he felt really sorry for me because I did not know the truth. 'Everyone,' he said, 'has to die one day, but it's the not knowing that's the worst.' Uncle Anil promised to contact his cousin, also in England, to find out the whereabouts of Dev and Mama. He had the phone number of a friend who might have been able to find out. I knew these were all false hopes, as maybe no one would really know of their whereabouts, or anything else.

Last month Christmas time and there were a few Indian Christians who were excited about celebrating this festival, and with the New Year just passed around the corner, I felt I should have phoned Charlie to wish her Happy Christmas and a prosperous New Year. This was what we had said to her every year as she would always pop in, or we would go round to hers. It had been a while so it was nice to talk to her once again even though it was a bit late for Merry Christmas. As I started to tell her about Mama's news there was a sadness in her voice. I then began to tell her about Rocky and what he did to me. It all came back to me. I was pregnant, *still*. She was shocked as to why I had taken all this and not done anything about it. What could I do? I told her there was only one thing left to do and that I would do it that week.

Later in the week I wrote to Mama again, telling her about my fears for her and what had happened to me and the state I was in. I knew that there would be no reply but I didn't want her to be able to say, 'Well, you never told me.'

That same week I took Suhaani Ma with me and we went to the lady doctor. I went in by myself while she sat outside. I had told her I had a lot of pain and so needed the lady doctor. The doctor told me that there was a greater chance of the 'friend' being the father rather than my husband. I told her I needed to get rid of it. She said it was very dangerous now as I was three months pregnant. She said she would give me a letter to take to the local hospital in the nearest town and they would be able to help me.

'Can't any of your Smarties, your tablets, help me?' I asked.

She smiled back at me, nodding politely.

Auntie Khushi, Suhaani Ma and I all went to the local hospital. It looked like a pharmacy office rather than a hospital. I told them to wait outside. I went in and gave the letter. They took me in and, as I lay on the bed, they put an ultrasound machine on my belly. I could see the baby alive and kicking. I insisted that I did not want to keep it, so they gave me a pill, before carrying out the procedure. After a while it was over. It – the baby – came out. I tried hard not to look but it was impossible. It was a boy, or so it looked to me. I know it seems insensitive, but I did look to see if it was a boy or a girl. Mind you, that really didn't matter anyway. I had got rid of the baby and that was that. It was a callous act on my part I know, but I definitely could not have kept the baby. It was not even because I was too young but because of who the father was – a father who had no permission to be the father to my child. I had not consented to him to father this baby.

Cold, lonely and heartless is how this all seemed. People think about it again and again but really I had already made the decision from the beginning. It was a part of life that I did not consent to having, so why should I have had to keep it? Especially for the rest of my life. What if it had turned out to look, and more worryingly behave, like Rocky? There was no way that, as Maansi advised, I could have lied for ever to Suhaan, telling him that the baby was his. That would have been unbearable to live with, and not fair on him. How could I tell Suhaan that *a quick 'romp' in the haystack*, a moment of lustful passion from Rocky, had left me facing my biggest regret: I had to have my baby killed.

I am not very religious but I still know enough to realise that I would never be forgiven for this sin. If I can take a life then so can God, the ruler of all lives, take mine, and he will without telling me. Whether I go to heaven or hell, I will still have to take the punishment for this sin. How would I be able to repay the life I had taken?

With all these thoughts running through my head and my heart, the feelings of guilt were making me cry and, as I left the surgery, Suhaani Ma and Auntie Khushi asked me why I was crying. I could not tell them and they didn't ask any more. During the journey back home, Auntie Khushi told Suhaani Ma that I had had a clean-out of the insides as I was in pain, and of course not getting pregnant either and that's why it took so long. Suhaani Ma thought it was a good idea. Little did she know that a clean-out meant cleansing every bit of life out of one's body, in my case.

I went straight to bed when I got home, and even though food was offered, I didn't feel like eating at all. Suhaan naturally wanted to make the most of me while I was not in a fighting spirit. He swiftly told me, rather than suggesting to me, that I take my clothes off. I told him I was in too much pain and not able. After all, I told him, he didn't want to ruin the chances of my becoming a mother. On hearing this he stopped his animal ways and left me alone, thank God!

Even though I looked pale and drained I did get up the next day and lay out in the sun, which did seem to cheer me up. I wrote a letter to Mama again, telling her what I had done the day before, and how I was guilt ridden, but how I was feeling fine and recovering. I told her not to worry. This is not what I actually meant. I wanted her to worry because no one else did, but then, neither did she!

Suhaan went to the post office and posted it for me, as I did not have the energy to go out. Naturally I knew that I would not get a reply, but as a dutiful daughter, I did my part. No letters were returned or answered. I often phoned Charlie but still there was no good news. She said she had a pile of my letters on the telephone table near the door in our house.

Spring came once again and showed its beautiful colours: the sun warmed the land, days became longer and the nights shorter. We had started to sleep outside again. It was not too muggy as it was in the summer, when some nights were so hot and sticky that we kept the fan on all night with a single sheet to cover us from the mosquitoes.

I kept writing the letters, but I did not know if my mother was alive or dead. I could not be sure as no one had heard from Dev, or at least that was what I was told. Rocky was the only one really close to Dev. He was probably the only one who knew the truth. Had he told me the truth, or was he paying me back because Auntie Khushi asked him about him and me. How could I get to the truth? I knew that deep down inside I had to find out. I had recovered from my abortion and things were back to normal. I had also got used to the fact that I had been raped by Rocky and there was nothing I could do to change that. I had to come to terms with it.

I knew that I would have to meet him again and find out the truth. When and how that would be, I didn't know. Moreover, would he tell me the truth? Who could get through to him? On the other hand I had to ask him myself; no one else would or could do it. After all, what had happened had happened to me. I was struggling with it all, obviously, but at least I knew that not much more could happen to me. What was left that could still be awaiting me? I had been raped, and circumstances had led me to abort my very first child. But even before these traumas I had been forced to marry a man who regularly forced me to do things I didn't want to do. The root of all these problems was the fact that I was brought here under false pretences, as far as I was concerned, and at a time when I, Sania Hema Craven, had lost my father for ever.

A Double Miracle

'BASTARD!'

'What?'

'Bastard,' I repeated.

'Who you calling—?'

'You. That is your real name, isn't it?'

'My name is Bhaskar, not the way you're pronouncing it.'

'Yes, of course, same thing – Bhaskar or bastard.'

'What does bastard mean? Is it a name?'

'Of course, for someone like you,' I laughingly said.

'Oh, I see,' replied Rocky.

'Why do they call you Rocky anyway?'

'It's because of the film, *Rocky*. I used to love fighting. That's why my uncle Dev gave me that name. So from Bhaskar, it became Rocky,' he explained. 'Is there no one home that you're on the roof and calling out to me?'

'Ma is resting and Suhaan has gone to get some vegetables. I need to see you, seriously. When and where?'

'You tell me. I know of only the animal stable where we met a few months ago.'

I yelled back quickly, 'No, not there. I know, come here tomorrow, at the same time.'

With that I got off the roof and sat in the courtyard planning what I was going to say to him, and, more importantly, how I could convince Suhaan to go out for me. Suhaani Ma was not a problem because siesta time is a must in the summer. She had to sleep for about two hours every day from two till four. I didn't sleep. Instead I listened to the radio or put my cassettes on. Music had become important to me, and yet in England it was always in the background. I was too busy there, but here I had all the time in the world.

The following day we all had breakfast and Suhaani Ma was preparing for lunch, which was around twelve o'clock. I insisted that, as it was nearly my seventeenth birthday, I wanted to eat samosas, pakoras and *ras malai*, as we did not celebrate my birthday last year. Plus I had been unwell and needed a treat for this birthday. After all, on my sixteenth birthday it should have been my biggest and best party but still I didn't ask for a treat. On this day I had to have it. Suhaan said, adamantly, that we could both go to the bazaar tomorrow, to which I said I was still not well enough to go, but said he must go and get the food later. He said it was not possible because if we left it any longer there would not be any pakoras left. As for the other items, they could only be bought from the nearest market town. I then told him that if he bought these things today and got back before five o'clock, we could do you-know-what, which he called 'kuch kuch', when Suhaani Ma was sleeping.

With that thought in mind he got ready instantly, and within seconds he was out with a big smile on his face. Suhaani Ma ate the leftovers from last night. As we were both to eat the food Suhaan was going to bring, she did not cook anything. At her usual time she went indoors, shut her door and went to sleep. I got up on the roof and could see Rocky approaching. He opened the gate and I told him to sit on the bed in the courtyard. We had to sit there so if anyone came I could say he had come to see Suhaan, making it look innocent.

'Who are you talking to, Sania?' Suhaani Ma called from her room. 'Who's here?'

'Oh, it's Rocky. He came to see Suhaan. He's going now.'

'OK, keep it down please. Offer him some water.'

I then explained to him that I needed to find out where my passport had vanished to and, because he was the closest to Dev, he would know. He might even have it. Whatever the situation I needed it or, if all else failed, I needed him to get the forms from town to get a new passport made. I could go with Auntie Khushi to get my photos done or with Suhaan, but no one must know or I would tell everyone what he did and would take action by telling the police, with the help of Suhaan. He then said he would see as he felt sorry for me. But as for telling Suhaan or the police, he was not worried as he would deny it all. He had made it clear that I did not have proof. He said there had to be something in it for him. He asked if we could be friends – in India, friendship between a girl and a boy normally means a girlfriend/boyfriend relationship. I was desperate, so I said yes. We were to meet the following day in the stables, but only when I could get away. He said he'd wait from two until four for me. With that he left.

No sooner had he gone than Suhaan came back. It was only a quarter to four, and even though I did not want to, I had to be faithful to my promise. Afterwards we both sat and ate the food. It was delicious – the food, not him.

Suhaani Ma rose and we offered her some of the food. She then asked about Rocky. I replied that he had come to see Suhaan about borrowing his tools for ploughing, and he would come back later. Suhaan didn't seem too concerned. In the evening, Suhaan went out, while I kept dwelling on what would happen on the following day. When Suhaan returned he asked me what Rocky had come for. I repeated what I had told him earlier. He replied that Rocky had come for something completely different and asked why I was lying. My face went red and I told him, muttering, that I must have got confused.

'Confused or lying? But why?'

'Yes, why? What reason would I have?'

'That's what I don't understand.'

'Why are you doubting me, Suhaan? Perhaps I should have woken Suhaani Ma, then there would have been no need to doubt me.'

'You should have. There's no need for a young girl to be talking to a man, especially Bhaskar.'

'Why especially Bhaskar?'

'Well, you should know. He's not married, is he? He is single and you are married. His mind works differently. All single men's minds work in the same way. They eye up women and have filthy thoughts. They have one-track minds.'

'Not all single men,' I pointed out.

'Yes, all single men,' he shouted.

I could sense the fury in his eyes, so I quietened down, only because I did not want to talk about Rocky any more. Also, I was hiding things myself, so pulling the wool over their eyes and not being truthful made me feel bad. I felt guilty, but had no way of escaping. I knew that, no matter what he dished out, I would need to keep him sweet. I had to keep my secrets.

The next day arrived soon enough and I knew I was playing with fire, but what other options did I have? Suhaan had made it perfectly clear that I was going nowhere. I knew that if I could get my passport and run away and leave India for England – run away from here, away from this life. I would never contact these people again. And I knew that, once I left, Suhaan would not treat me the way Dev treated us. He had a human side to him, unlike Dev.

I tried to send Suhaan out without making it obvious, but he just did not go. I had an appointment with someone but could not get away. I then said that I was going out to Maansi's, but he told me to stay as he was at home and we could talk. His 'talk' was not with words, but action, in bed, and that's exactly what happened. The following day was the same as he spent siesta time chopping wood in the yard. That day, the action was with tree trunks rather than me. Chopped wood was a necessity here as it was used for fires for cooking. Wood was plentiful.

Over the next couple of days, I still couldn't get away. I was busy being a perfect host to the women who came to visit us. Days had gone by and I was getting worried that Rocky may have thought that I was standing him up deliberately. On the sixth day the coast was clear, so I went.

He was standing there, making it obvious that he was waiting for someone. There was no one looking, so I ran quickly into the stable. He followed, and then we both stood there looking at one another. I looked at him with hatred; he looked at me with delight. The first thing that came into his mind was to hurry as someone might come in. He told me to get my clothes off, and quickly do what we came here to do. This infuriated me even more, and then I started to tell him that it was my passport I wanted, not sex.

He knew that he had the upper hand and, with much abuse, raved on about how nothing was free. I stood, silent. He then calmed down and moved closer, telling me that he had liked me since day one and if I pleased him then he would please me. I asked him to spell out exactly what he was going to do to please me. He said, 'Find your passport, or get you a new one.' He promised on his uncle Dev's life. I had to honour my end of the bargain and so I did. It was the same place as before, but this time there was no blood, sweat or tears, just humiliation. I felt dirty and cheap, but I was desperate, and desperate times call for desperate measures. I closed my eyes in disgust but he wanted me to keep my eyes open, to see everything.

Afterwards I went home and straight into the shower room to wash, but at that moment I heard Suhaan asking what I was doing. Without thinking I replied that I was taking a shower. He then told me not to be daft and have a shower in the morning. After all, why have a shower without a reason? For him, the only good reason was after sex. He added that I had already had one this morning so, like an obedient wife, I came straight out so that he would not suspect anything. Being hot and sticky due to the hot weather were no real reasons for having a shower as far as he was concerned. I didn't care about anything except getting my passport.

I had missed a period and knew that I was pregnant again. This time I knew that my husband was the father of the child and not Rocky as I was sinful with him just after that. Just as well really, as who knows how that would have turned out. I also felt that getting pregnant so quickly, and at such a young age, was a punishment handed down to me for the taking of a life; that I had sinned at my very young, tender age. I had only turned seventeen a few days before and celebrated it by having snacks and committing adultery. It was shameful. This year I had deliberately ignored Mama's birthday, as the year before it had caused me so much pain being unsure whether she was alive or dead. It was less painful to just forget her as she had me. How could I have done such a demeaning thing at such a tender age? I was still a child at school, or so I should have been. Instead I was creating sins for myself. Why couldn't I just accept my lot and get on with my life? Now I was seventeen I was to become a mother. This would make it much harder to escape, but I could not kill another life, and the Smarties had not done their job very well.

By April the following year I would have had my child. I would be four months away from being eighteen. I was growing up and time was moving so slowly. Time in England had always gone fast. At Christmas I phoned

Charlie again, even though she had phoned me quite a few times before. I told her I was pregnant and that I was also seeing Rocky in the hope of getting my passport. She tried to talk me out of it, but my mission was not complete.

By this time I was five months pregnant and looking very weak and thin. For the first four months I did not tell anyone, but then Suhaani Ma figured it out, and I admitted it to be the truth. They were amazed at why I didn't tell them both. They were ecstatic with joy. Everyone that heard came to congratulate them both on the future baby to be born into the family. They gave sweetmeats to visitors and talked about names, clothes and all manner of baby things. I was still on a mission, a failing one at that, to get my passport. Rocky and I would meet once a week, sometimes once every fortnight, and nearer the new year, as I became heavier and heavier, it was once a month.

After January we did not meet any more as I was too heavy and could not walk around without attracting attention to myself. I told Rocky that there was no space for anything else to go up there. For a thin girl, my bump was quite big. It was all you could see. Throughout the pregnancy I had not visited the lady doctor, or gone for a check-up, as they were not routine.

March hurried along, and so did the flowers and the warmth – all welcoming signs for someone who could not walk as fast as before. My strides were slower and much heavier. I still kept meeting Maansi, and one day, as we were talking about how I would be stuck at home more once the baby arrived, she asked, 'Where do you do you-know-what with Rocky?'

'In the stable.'

'Show me?'

We went in. A horse was tied up. Maansi started giggling and asked, 'Is Rocky's thingy bigger than the horse's?'

'What?'

'Did you know, Sania, that a horse's thingy, his willy, is the biggest of all. If it ever goes inside a woman she would die. It would reach up to her throat!' Maansi could still be so childish and crude, but she made me laugh. We both sat down on a bale of hay next to the horse, giggling and joking. Then she dared me to touch his thingy and see if it was as warm and big as Rocky's. After all, the horse and Rocky were both big. I couldn't resist a dare and so I neared myself beside the horse and reached my arm under him. I was sitting practically underneath the big animal. All of a sudden the horse bolted, threw out his leg against my stomach making me lose my balance on the bale. I fell back and landed in manure. Maansi pulled and tugged at me, helping me get back on my feet. I was still scared of getting hurt again as the horse was still standing there, but he just looked on. I put my hands on the floor, in the muck, and got up.

As I plodded slowly home with Maansi I knew that all was not well, and not because I stunk so badly. As soon as we got to our gate Maansi started shouting, 'Suhaani Ma, come quickly. I've had the baby. No, no, tut, I mean Sania Madam's had her baby.'

Suhaani Ma hurried towards us. 'Where and when?'

'No, having it, you know, now having IT.'

'It?'

'Yes, Suhaani Ma.'

She grabbed me and took me inside and onto the bed. She told Maansi to get the clean towels, and then fetch Auntie Malini from her house. My pain was getting worse. I felt as if something, I supposed it was the baby, was actually coming out from my behind, with such excruciating pain. I thought it was supposed to come out from near the front, not the back, but then I had never given birth to a baby before. Suhaani Ma was busy cleaning the horse muck off me and my clothes. I thought the whole house would stink of it. Slowly but surely the pains eased a bit and Suhaani Ma said that was good. She told me to stay in bed to stop the contractions as there was still a month to go yet. I needed to go to the toilet, and Maansi helped me. I told her, while I was on the toilet in a squatting position, she must go and tell her mother or else she'd worry. She must have run all the way there and back.

A few minutes later Auntie Khushi and Maansi came back and shouted, 'Are you OK in there?'

'No, Maansi. I think the baby is coming out!'

'Let me in, Sania.'

'I am in too much pain to open the lock.'

'Don't worry, I can climb over, no problem.'

And so she did without any hesitation – a real tomboy. She got me up, pulled my sari straight and took me into the room once again. Auntie Malini was prepared for me already. She kept saying, 'We're ready for you.' I could not see any doctors or nurses though. She told me to have some hot milk with almonds. I had a sip. I could taste ginger in it as well. Maansi quickly grabbed it and gulped it down. She said it would hurry the baby along as nothing would stop it from coming now. She said that by sitting on my feet it would help the baby push down. So I placed my feet on the bricks she had laid out on the floor and crouched, Maansi sat in that position also right in front of me as if she was also giving birth. Underneath was mud and sand so they could brush away whatever was not needed. I did as I was told. It was not comfortable sitting like that but a quick birth was better than a slow one.

'Please just hurry it along, Suhaani Ma,' I pleaded, 'as I'm in too much pain. Just take it out.'

'How can we take the baby out? It will come in its own time.'

'Just breathe, child,' said Auntie Khushi. Maansi started her breathing. Auntie Khushi just nodded her head.

I tried breathing, puffing and panting but no luck: it was still too painful. Maansi was not in pain but she was still busy practising her breathing.

'It's OK, baby's coming,' said Auntie Malini.

'Where?' shouted Maansi excitedly.

'You stupid girl, where do you think? Now clear off, this is not for kids!'

'Kids? Kids? The only kid is coming, so don't look at me!' she said, puffing and panting.

A little while later, Maansi had calmed down.

'Sorry, I didn't think…'

'Yes, that'd be right,' chuckled Auntie Malini.

'Why don't you, Maansi, go and play with the stones outside?'

'And miss this, Auntie Malini? No thanks. This is more fun.'

'This is not fun,' I said through gritted teeth. 'I'm in so much pain.'

'Child, having children is never easy. Be brave,' said Auntie Khushi. 'It has only been four hours. Be patient child.'

Maansi then asked, 'Shall I go and get Cousin Suhaan?'

'Tut-tut, what will he do here? It's not something for men,' replied Suhaani Ma quickly.

I suddenly felt an urge to push.

'Ah… ah… push child, but not too hard,' began Auntie Khushi, 'or you'll tear.'

Maansi looked up. 'Tear from where?'

'Not you Maansi, I'm talking to Sania. Now push gently,' continued Auntie Khushi. 'We are holding you, don't worry, we won't let you go. Lean on us…'

I pushed, but nothing. The pain was still intense.

'Try again when you feel you must, not before that. Ready now, a big push, pant now… And push, push…'

I pushed again. I thought I might pass out from the pain. I felt a movement and then…

'Oh, the good Lord has given you a healthy boy!' announced Auntie Khushi.

'Oh, I'm in so much pain,' I muttered, crying and sobbing.

'It's OK now, it's over. Rest – sleep if you can.'

By that time I was already drowsy, as if I had the drowsy cough syrup Father sometimes gave me before bed. After a short while, my pains came back and I knew something was wrong.

'You makeshift midwives have done something wrong,' I started shouting. 'I am in a lot of pain again. You've messed up, you stupid illiterate women don't know anything… stupid women, hope you die, stupid, stupid women…'

'For God's sake, calm down.'

'No, I won't, I won't… Ah, ah… I feel like pushing again.'

'Go to sleep,' said Suhaani Ma. 'It's nothing, it's over.'

'I'm telling you, I'm in pain. You've done something wrong, you and this stupid woman.'

All of a sudden Auntie Malini lifted my sari and said quickly, 'She's right. The child is right.'

'Have we done something wrong? Oh no, I'll never forgive myself.'

'No, Suhaani Ma, there's another baby on the way!'

'What? I'm having another one? Breathe… breathe…'

'Not you, you stupid child, Maansi! I'm telling Sania. Get lost from here!'

I pushed again, and panted. Push, pant, push, pant… Just over ten minutes later the second baby arrived.

'It's a miracle, Suhaani Ma. You have two grandsons! Congratulations!'

A double miracle. My double miracle.

My Beloved's Last Breath

FOR THE FIRST six weeks of having the boys I was not allowed out of the house, and was asked to rest most of the time, as this was traditional. I breastfed them both and in between, bottle-fed them too. Suhaan would at times give them goat's or cow's milk. They were quite small and yet so perfect. There was more of me in them but they did have their father's likeness as well. Suhaan was like an uglier version of Kurt Russell, and so the boys had their father's nose and dimple in the chin. The older one had a mole on the left side of his neck and the younger had a tiny mole on the bottom of his jaw on the right-hand side. Apart from this they looked identical and so gorgeous.

I was fair skinned, and Suhaan dark. Thank goodness, I thought, that the boys were fair like me. Suhaani Ma chose their names, did all the Hindu rituals and got all their goods including clothes. She bathed them, put them to sleep and woke up for them in the night as well.

The six weeks were full of people coming and going and yet it was as if I was a prisoner in my own home. I could not step outside. After the sixth week I was told to shower, change clothes, remove all my body hair (except that on my head), and with that, the days of new motherhood were officially over. The boys had to have their heads shaved, have black thread tied on their wrist, a small black dot on their foreheads and black eye pencil, like kohl, around their eyes. With all this they could have easily been mistaken for twin girls.

Suhaani Ma was no longer energetic and full of life. She had lost a lot of weight and felt thirsty often. She insisted that it was nothing and could have been just the fact that she overdid things with the house, visitors and the babies, and was feeling run down. Suhaan however called the doctor in and he told her she may have become diabetic. She said she had heard of it but never had anyone in the family experienced it before. She persisted that it could not be, so he asked her to pass some urine over a stick to test for it. She did so, and then he showed her the result. She didn't believe it, so he asked me to do the same on a stick as comparison. Now she believed it. He gave her an injection straight away and told her to take a tablet three times a day with each meal.

With this condition, she seemed to stop doing the housework altogether, and the most she did with the boys was to carry them or feed them with a bottle. Now, through no fault of hers, everything was on my shoulders: the three boys, Suhaani Ma, the house, the cooking, cleaning and the guests. I asked her to go and visit her sister and her family, as this was the only family she had left, apart from Suhaan and her grandsons. She would often go, as they were in the same village, stay the day there and come back in the evening.

I had tried to do all I could for her as she had been really good to me: massaging her back and feet for her, giving her an Indian head rub as well, but all that was only temporary. My problems had just begun and I hardly had any time to think about them. I got up at six o'clock in the morning to milk the cow and used that milk to make breakfast tea and feed the boys. I then made breakfast for mother and son – both had *parathas* – cleaned and tidied up. Then I changed the boys, bathing them only when it was warm enough. After this I got dinner ready for twelve o'clock, washed and tidied and fed the boys again before they slept in the afternoon. While they slept I did the clothes, washed and ironed, and then made tea. I then got the food ready again for the evening meal. It was just as well that Suhaan fed and cleaned the animals himself.

There were days when I would just drop onto the bed with exhaustion, no energy for anything. Mind you, Suhaan still had the energy to be animal-like. Many a time I would not shower if it was not warm, and it was so tedious warming a bit of water to bathe in; I only had the patience to warm it for the boys. In between their crying and attention seeking, I was fed up and lonely as hell. I had absolutely no time for myself. Suhaan did not help with the boys as he said it was the mother's job to raise and nurture the children.

There were times when I had a high temperature and felt unable to get up, but still he persisted in not helping, saying he had things to do. Doing chores for his twins were not a priority, so I had to do them. They were my priority now. I was responsible for them full-time. Maansi used to come but only for a short while for she had the responsibility of looking after her siblings and the house. When she did come it was a joy to have her as she laughed and played with them both. I think she felt more for the little twin as he was very small.

One day Rocky came to the house.

'We don't see you out and about any more, Sania,' he stated.

'No, you wouldn't as I don't have the time any more, Bhaskar.'

'Well, if there's anything I can do to help?'

'You've helped already. That's why I'm in a mess. I don't need your help any more.'

'What are you saying, child,' shouted Suhaani Ma.

'Oh, I'm sorry, Bhaskar, I'm just tired,' I said quickly, just to keep the peace and save any argument. But I knew what he meant very well; I was not seeing him any more. Day in, day out, I was busy all the time, but when I looked at my boys, somehow it all seemed worthwhile. When the boys were playing happily Suhaan would hold them and play with them, but as soon as they started to cry he would hand them over to me. So typical.

There were many days when I would ask him to help, but instead he would go out with his friends, leaving me crying through desperation. I was growing further and further away from him. I would get the boys and put them both on either side of me and cry myself to sleep. But no matter how bad things got I always told them that I loved them and sealed it with a kiss.

That year on my birthday I had turned eighteen and no one even remembered, so I told my boys and they gave me a kiss each, even though they were only five months old. October was upon us once again and it was chilly in the mornings and evenings. It was difficult keeping the boys warm. I did not want to bathe them but the youngest had vomited, and Suhaan told me to bathe him. I explained it was too cold but he insisted that it was fine. He said it was just me, always cold, because I came from a cold country and the cold was in my body.

I bathed both of them in the sunshine during the day as it was colder inside. I wrapped them up after dressing them, but somehow the youngest seemed too relaxed. I kept telling Suhaan that something was wrong, but he kept saying he was fine. Suhaani Ma said if Suhaan says he's fine, he must be fine, after all, he is his father. That night the little one did not eat or take his bottle. My fears got worse. During the night I kept waking up to see him but he was asleep all of the time. My gut feeling told me that he was not well. The night passed and morning came, and as I went to get the milk, the boys were still asleep.

After milking the cow, as I came in from the gate, I could hear the older one crying. Suhaan had not heard as he was now sleeping in the big room. There was only room for one bed in our room, and it was the warmest room, so the boys and I slept in there. Still, there was no way that he could not have heard, but then they do say that being asleep is the same as being dead. The boys were usually fast asleep at this time of the morning. Why had he woken up today? I put the pail of milk down in the hatch quickly, and ran to my room. He had fallen off the bed and that's why he was crying. I picked him up and started to cry myself as I felt sorry for him. I looked at him thoroughly but he didn't seem to be hurt, bruised or sore. I thought, *It's just the shock of falling*, but then it was my fault. However, I had no choice but to leave the room. The little one was still fast asleep.

'Hey, wake up baby. Why didn't you take care of your big brother? Look he fell over.'

He wouldn't wake up. I put the older one in his father's bed and started to make tea. After breakfast I woke the little one up but his eyes just did not look right. I kept saying that he wasn't well, and when Suhaani Ma saw his eyes she told Suhaan to go and get the doctor. She said the child looked as if he had pneumonia. *Oh no, that's my fault*, I thought. *I bathed him yesterday and since then he has not been well*. Feelings of guilt circled my head until the doctor came. He took one look at him, and without examining him further, took a syringe out from his bag.

'What the bloody hell are you doing with this?' I demanded.

'I'm going to make your child better. He has a cold. He'll be fine after this, believe me.'

'Are you sure?' I blurted out as my anger died down.

He nodded politely.

My baby didn't even cry when the needle went in. The doctor told Suhaan to get some medicine he had prescribed. For the rest of that day my boy didn't look well, but by the evening he looked much better. Maybe the medicine worked, I said to Suhaan that maybe being near death had relieved him of all his pains, but then we did not know that. I felt relieved because he was looking better, and that night, because I did not want to see anything bad any more, I asked Suhaan to sleep with us, and he did: myself and the little one on one side, Suhaan and the big one on the other.

It was still dark when I was woken up by a bad dream. My little one was calling me. I looked at the clock – it was 3 a.m. I looked at him: he was breathing his last breaths for his mother before dying. *My beloved's last breath.* He was hoping that I would wake up and meet him before he went to God. I started crying loudly and took him into my arms, kissing him and asking him to talk to me and smile, but his pupils seems to dilate more and more. It was almost like watching a ghost child, not a real child. He was silent, not feeling, not smiling, not anything – lifeless. He didn't look at me, but I was looking clearly into his eyes.

I shouted for Suhaan to get up. He did instantly, putting the lamp on. He started to beat his hands on his head, shouting and crying. Suhaani Ma rushed in, yelling at the scene. She silenced him and left. Soon people started gathering round, and then the doctor came, the same one as before.

My baby's eyes stared at me. I tried to close them as I put my face against his beautiful, sweet-smelling breath, as he took his last deep breath, and then lay peacefully, yet lifelessly, in my arms. My eyes just would not stop crying. This crying was from the heart, from deep, deep down inside. I looked at Suhaan. He was crying, his eyes and nose were dripping. He made no attempt to wipe them. He was very sad; I had never seen him like this, ever.

My big boy sat on the bed watching us, smiling all the while. He didn't utter a word, a giggle or a sigh. I had no idea how long I or Suhaan had been crying until I noticed the daylight and someone turning out the lamp. Someone asked me to put the baby on the bed so we could all move outside. I moved but refused to put the baby down. He had been in my arms for hours yet I had hardly felt his weight. He was seven months old yet no burden in his mother's arms.

There was no breakfast, no food, just tears and loud crying in the house. Usually it would be only me crying. Maansi came with Auntie Khushi, and so did the rest of the family. Maansi and Auntie Khushi cuddled me but I only had arms for my boy.

Auntie Khushi took him from me, slowly, to bathe him, and then wrapped him in a white cloth. He looked just like Papa, but a tiny version. I was not allowed to touch him or carry him any more as he had now been purified and the soul had left the body and gone to heaven – all babies go straight to heaven. I kept touching him still, but no longer had him in my arms. I tried to close his eyes but they wouldn't. Someone kept saying, 'Put some honey on his eyes to close them.' I told them to leave him alone.

Auntie Khushi covered my head as the men carried the bed – the bed that they bathed him on, the one we slept on every night – with my boy on it, wrapped up as if he were bandaged. We walked to our graveyard near the stable. A grave was already waiting for him. A man climbed into it and laid my boy to sleep in there, on the soil, to rest for eternity.

Rocky put in a wooden panel after leaving a three-foot gap, and then asked Suhaan to tell me to put the first bit of soil in the grave. I stared at the wooden panel. Down below this was my baby. I could no longer see him. He would not need to rise and sit for questioning on the day of judgement as adults have to. Suhaan took my hand and made me grab some soil and together we threw it onto the plank.

'Take care of my baby,' I said through my tears, 'he's yours now Papa.'

Everyone else offered prayers after the head of the temple recited verses from the holy book. Next, everyone threw soil and then, with a shovel, the grave was all covered up into a neat little cot where my boy would sleep for ever.

'Why have you covered him up? Let me get him, he'll be hungry now,' I yelled hysterically, as Suhaan stopped me from removing the mud. I sat there for a long time, and so did many others offering prayers. It was getting dark, and at that time I realised it was evening. Auntie Khushi carried my big boy all the time. I picked him up and walked home. I slept with my boy on that same bed. The others were still there, asking me to eat, drink and wash. I did not reply. I had never been so silent before, not even at my wedding or my mother's. I kept stroking the bed and could see him so clearly there with me.

I awoke the next morning as if from a bad dream, but it was reality, as was the day before. The previous night, my son had woken me up so that his mother could see him alive for the last time, so I could smell and feel his last dying breaths. I cuddled my big boy tightly, saying to him, 'Stay close son, don't leave Mummy.'

Suhaan had also slept with me but he behaved himself. He had crept into bed when it was very late, and silently turned the other way and dozed off.

I got up, went to the toilet, washed my hands and face and brushed my teeth. I didn't have a shower, didn't comb my hair, didn't change my clothes or apply make-up. Everyone kept saying things like 'get her to open up and talk as it will damage her', 'it will make her ill – then who will look after the child?', 'she's a mother; she has responsibilities', 'please, child, eat or at least drink some tea'. I did not eat anything. I sat in a trance carrying my son. When he needed something done, Auntie Khushi did it. Local women came, did the cleaning and cooked, then tidied up and sat with us until dark. I sat in the graveyard for the majority of the day.

When it got dark I went to sleep, again with my son. The following day it was the same routine, but Auntie Khushi did force me to eat as it was the third day of the death, the third day of reciting payers all day long, the third day of mourning. My eyes had dried up. Even though I still wanted to cry, I just couldn't. I remember women saying to me, 'Don't cry. The child's soul does not rest while the mother is crying.' I had ignored them for the past two days, but this time, even though I wasn't actually crying, my eyes still looked like it.

'Shut up – stop saying that,' I said to them. 'Have you just buried your son?'

In response to that they were quiet and sympathised. Every day men and women came, some ate and sat all day making idle conversation. This carried on for two weeks and finally I cracked. I cried so much just thinking of my baby and what would remain of him in the ground; just bones, just his tiny skeleton. Everyone said that I must shower; it had been two weeks. Auntie Khushi had been such a good friend, she had been looking after my son so well. Some nights she slept in the house with us too. She made me go and have a shower, and so I did. She also made me change my clothes as they were full of mud from the grave.

As I sat there in the sun with my hair tangled by the lack of combing over the two weeks, she sat and combed it for me. It reached the bed, right down to my backside. How

Mama would have been proud of me – long, straight, tangle-free hair. Is this how she felt when Papa died, as I was feeling? Is that why she was so hard on me? But I wanted to stay close to my son, while she had kept me at arm's length.

Eventually, less and less people came and so things were getting back to normal again. Instead of staying all day at the grave, I used to go home quite a lot, and then return to the grave. Suhaan was not his usual self yet either. He didn't go to the bazaar to see his friends or go into town. He would spend a lot of time at home, sitting, thinking, going to the graveyard, doing a few chores around the home. But throughout the two weeks we never shared our feelings, the pain, anger or frustration. We slept together quietly.

A month had gone by and the doctor who visited us came to give me the death certificate. I glanced at it – the verdict said pneumonia. I got up, fetched the medicines he had prescribed and a spoon. I put the medicine in the spoon and shouted, 'Here, give him this, you said. He only caught a cold. Suhaani Ma told you that it was pneumonia. You said that he'd be fine. We believed you, we trusted you, otherwise we could have taken him to hospital where he could have got better. You treated him for the wrong thing, you bastard. Are you a real doctor or are you just an illiterate, *pendoo*, Indian freshy with no education whatsoever? Now drink this medicine.'

I started spilling the medicine over him and forcing it in his mouth, shouting, 'I hope your children die as well. I hope you suffer like me. I hope you don't get to even feel your children's last breath. I hope your wife throws you out…', all the while crying. Suhaan came and made me sit down on the bed and apologised to him.

'Don't apologise to him from me. No one is safe here because everyone knows nothing: no school, no college, no fun, no knowledge… all bloody *pendoos*, all freshies.'

Suhaan just stood there, silent, watching me with amazement, but also with pain. He knew I had included him in that tirade as well, after all he was not educated either. He had spent most of his time playing volleyball and cricket with the boys rather than going to school. To boys, it seemed, education was only important to the very few who appreciated life and had ambition. The rest want to spend their time with friends, no worries or cares about where the money was coming from, or of course go to England as a fiancée or husband and do the jobs others would not – this was their life.

Mothers and Daughters, Sisters and Wives

I HAD ABORTED a child, and so I had been punished by God. It was all fair and square now. The pain I had caused the unborn child I then felt when my boy died. The good Lord had paid me back, but my papa would have said, 'No, child, never say that. Jesus died for us. The good Lord would never take any of his people as punishment. He forgives everyone.'

Since the death of my boy I had written to my mother twice: once to tell her of his death, the death of her grandson, and to tell her about the burial, how he was laid to rest; then secondly to let her know that, as she had never replied I may never write to her again. It was almost a goodbye letter.

It was Christmas time again and you may wonder why was Christmas so important to me. I was half English and my papa had celebrated Christmas. I phoned Charlie and, as usual, wished her a Happy Christmas. However she seemed to know straight away that something was wrong. I told her the whole story, or rather the nightmare, of losing my boy. I was crying and talking at the same time. She listened and cried and hardly uttered a word. She said that she wished there was something she could do to take my pain away but, alas, there was nothing anyone could do.

In January we had decided upon putting a plaque on the grave. It read:

A plaque to remember the birth of two inseparable boys, who came into this world together on 21 March 1983, and yet the good Lord decided to separate them by taking one away on 20 October 1983, just seven months old. Always in our hearts and will always be seen alive through the eyes of his brother. Love you always, you'll always be missed, Kez Suhaan Rana, by your parents, Suhaan Rana, Sania Hema Craven, and your twin brother, Haari.

A builder was called and we, the family members, went into the graveyard to have the grave cemented and the plaque fitted near the head. Once finished, it somehow looked complete and not new any more. It seemed to blend in with all the other graves. Kez had become just like the rest, asleep, so fast asleep, resting in peace for always. All the family were invited to offer final prayers, along with the *Baba Ji*, the local priest, who was the head of the place of worship here. He recited his knowledge, offering a peaceful and eternal heaven for Kez, and patience and comfort for his parents to carry on in life.

A caterer from our village, with no qualifications but with life experiences – wiping his nose on his shirt, sweat dripping into the pots – came to do all the cooking and everyone ate to their heart's content, except for Suhaan and me. He was looking sad and needed comfort like me, but I could not give him anything he needed because I was caught up in my own grief and loneliness.

From this day onwards everyone in the family seemed to put the death in the past and started to live their normal lives again. To some extent so did I. Suhaani Ma had told me to go and spend time with Maansi again, as it would take my mind off the grief, so I did, but this time two of us went – Haari and his mother. He was my only pride and joy, and someone who I had to live for.

We didn't sit on the tree branch any more as it was a bit dangerous, and I certainly did not go into the stable either, not for the horse or for Rocky. We sat on a blanket on the floor, all three of us, and talked for at least two hours every day.

One day I asked Maansi how Maya was related to Dev, as that was how she had introduced herself to me. Maya had come with Maansi most days during our mourning period and had stayed for quite a while, and unlike some women who were chatting, she would remain quiet. She seemed like a girl who had the weight of the world on her shoulders, a bit like me. Maansi was as truthful as you could get: if anyone asked her anything she would either say she was not allowed to speak of it, or just tell you the truth as she knew it.

So, tell me the truth she did. Maya was indeed Dev's relative. She was his niece, and in fact Rocky's sister. This 29-year-old woman, who looked not a day older than twenty, hung around with Maansi because, apart from Auntie Khushi, no one else really talked to her a lot. Maansi did not care who you were or what you did. She never judged anyone. Maya's story went back as least ten years when her mother, Alisha, was still alive and came to her brother Dev to live out the final few days of her life.

As a young woman, Alisha had been sent away by Dev when she disgraced her family. She was a bit of a bright spark and had convinced everyone that she should be allowed to go to town to study in a college. Study she did, but she also fell in love with a Sikh boy called Aman, and with the clash of religions and caste (she was a Hindu Punjabi), everyone was against it. She never returned home after that and no one mentioned her name either. She did, however, finish her studies successfully, and was friends with Aman until their marriage after her studies. She found it very hard, coping without a family, as we were told by people who said they had met her in the city. Soon after she had had her first child, Milli, Dev went to her saying he wanted to reconcile. No one really knew what happened to Aman. While he was practising as a doctor he seemed to have disappeared. There was no formal cancellation of his practice at the hospital or any explanation to Alisha either.

There was no dead body found so there was no proof of what had happened exactly, but it all occurred when Dev started visiting Alisha. Finally, he convinced Alisha to return home for Milli's sake, and so she did. All the while she was at home she kept blaming Dev for Aman's disappearance, saying he was responsible and even that he had had him killed. Other times she accused him of having Aman transferred far away with a promise of never returning and paying him handsomely for it. Maybe he was dead, but there was no proof of anything.

Dev would try to talk to her about re-marrying and how he was fixing her up with someone. She kept refusing and wanted to bring up Milli – the love that she was given by Aman – by herself. Finally she left one day without telling anyone, then wrote to explain that she was fine and staying where she used to live with Aman in case he ever came back. He would know where to find her. Dev's father told him to let it be and let her live her life as she wanted to.

A year went by and once again Dev came back from the city with Alisha, but this time she had a two-year-old Milli and a baby boy a few months old. The only explanation she gave was that she never remarried or saw Aman again, but Dev blackened her name further by saying that she had been a prostitute to earn easy money to raise her children and no one knew who the father was. She was in a bad way and she didn't look well. She looked as if she was tired of life; as if there was no more struggle left in her any more, especially against Dev. As her father was dead now she had no one who would side with her. Dev was her sole caretaker, being her elder brother.

Milli grew up into beautiful, gentle child, while Bhaskar, her brother, became a gruesome, rough child. However much Auntie Khushi tried to help her, she would keep her distance for she knew that she was Dev's wife and resented her. Dev was scared of Alisha running off again so after a few months he married her off to a local man who had had a family from before. He took her in and looked after her well, and she seemed happy enough. His children, her step-children, were all married and as a family they all got on well. Everything seemed good except for her health. She seemed to go downhill all the time and had lost the will to live without her Aman.

Alisha's husband, Thiloo, was obviously more of a father figure to her as far as his age was concerned, and had seemed well, until suddenly one evening he had a heart attack, and by the time they thought of taking him to the town he had passed away peacefully. It was then that she returned to Dev, to live out her last days. She also knew that Milli, Aman's daughter and Bhaskar, her child from the town, and Maya, Thiloo's child, all needed to be looked after so she left them with Dev and Khushi. She died peacefully knowing that they were with the only family she had. She passed away overnight and, as the doctor came, requested by Dev, he said that she had had cancer for a long time, and he knew about it. She had requested that the doctor tell no one but her Aman, if ever it were possible, which it wasn't. The doctor said that without him she had lost the will to live, let alone fight.

Auntie Khushi brought up the children as best she could, like her own. Milli was ambitious like her mother and wanted to study. After much convincing from Khushi, Dev finally let Milli go to town to study. He would, however, drop her and pick her up every day, and sometimes just sent the van and driver for her. One day he went himself and he saw her talking to a boy outside the college. He enquired about it, but she denied talking to him because she knew it was not allowed by Dev's rules. He started to mistrust her and became obsessed with trying to catch her out, convinced that she was having an affair and had turned like her own mother. One day he did catch her talking to a boy and there was hell at home that day. However she promised never to speak to him again, but deep down inside he didn't trust her any more. He vowed that if he ever saw that same boy, or any boy with her, he would beat him to death and kill her.

Once again he found her talking to another boy and she tried to convince him that he was merely another student. He was not convinced. He beat the boy and, after bringing her home, he beat her as all. She kept saying she was innocent, and Auntie Khushi sided with her. She tried to calm both sides down. Dev was still angry, but more disappointed as he felt that she had turned out like her mother, and said, 'She has bad blood running through her veins – her father's blood.' Milli couldn't believe that there would now be no college and she would only remain at home, and that at the nearest opportunity a wedding would be arranged for her. She decided her own destiny. She took an overdose of painkillers and ended her own life.

Everyone was sleeping in the same room and yet Milli managed to take the tablets and die without anyone noticing. In the morning they found her; her mouth was foaming with spit. She was laid to rest next to her mother, Alisha. *Mother and daughter, side by side.* From this point onwards Dev started to take more care of Bhaskar, even though at the beginning as he was the 'bastard' child, or so Dev used to say. However, maybe he felt responsible for Milli's death. Dev and Bhaskar would spend a lot of time out in the bazaar, leaving Maya alone and craving attention. And attention she got from a local boy, who was a Muslim. This relationship would never be allowed. As everyone so far had only paid attention, first to Milli and then to Bhaskar, Maya had planned things for herself. She convinced Dev to let her go to the local village school and carried on meeting the Muslim boy, Kaif Ali.

Finally, she told Auntie Khushi about the Muslim boy, who told Dev. He told her it could never be. She kept saying she loved him with all her heart. He told her that she was too young to know about what was right or wrong, let alone about love. She was immature and he felt that she was too naïve to know, or even make a decision, especially as she was only sixteen. She had, of course, liked Kaif Ali before then and met him regularly but never got found out. He had declared his love to her by telling her that the very first time he set his eyes on her he loved her.

Milli had been sensible and sensitive, but Maya was loud, immature and easily influenced by friends and not family. She knew that no one at home would accept him for he was a Muslim and, in order to marry him, she would have to leave her religion as well, which no family member would accept. This conflict at home made her more aggressive and at times hard to handle. She wanted to accept his proposal of marriage but there was no way the family would. Even Auntie Khushi told her it could never be.

These two families were worlds apart in religion but living together in the same village. He was a boy who was dominated by his parents and was often physically abused by his father as a way of making him tame – Kaif Ali was a bit of a bad boy: he smoked, used drugs, missed school, was bad-tempered, had a violent streak and was full of resentment in life in general due to his very strict control by his parents. Personality-wise, Kaif Ali and Maya were opposites.

One day Maya was told that Kaif Ali had, under his parents' instruction, got married to their choice of bride. She replied that she knew and that was all her family's fault. If they had allowed her to marry him, he would not have got married elsewhere. She resented Dev even more, but Dev didn't want to be too controlling with her in case she did the same thing as Milli. Finally, Dev convinced her to go and stay with Khushi's family so she would have time to think about things. They welcomed her as their own. She kept saying she loved Kaif Ali, and Kaif Ali still said that he loved her, but was living with his wife, Jia Khan Ali. Before Maya left, she told Dev that she would never disgrace him or herself, but would only marry Kaif Ali, and would wait all her life for him and the family's blessings. To date she still lives with Khushi's family and has not married. She still swore she loved only Kaif Ali and would do so until death.

'With all this happening to Milli and Maya, Bhaskar said he would never get involved in love or marriage.'

'Oh goodness, Maansi, what a sad story,' I sighed.

'Yes, indeed it is.'

'How do you know all this?'

'Well, Auntie Khushi of course.'

'Oh my God.'

'And guess what: everyone says that Kaif Ali has no children, and Auntie Khushi says that maybe he only married Jia for the sake of his parents and has not taken her with his heart, so they don't do you know what.'

'How come Maya doesn't come here often? After all, I've only seen her here now for the first time,' I asked.

'Well, you know that normally girls live with their parents and, ideally, a father figure, which was Dev. Even though he was really good with Maya, buying her whatever she wanted, she always had this resentment towards him because of Kaif Ali. She wouldn't come often, and the only time she would come was when Dev or Auntie Khushi would go and get her to come and stay. Now, she said she had heard that Dev was no longer here and so she decided to come and stay. I think this time she will stay for good. Bhaskar has asked her to stay with him as he says he has no real family left.'

'Do you think she will marry?'

'I really don't think so. You know how pretty she is, and, my God, Milli was even more beautiful. She had gorgeous, light-coloured eyes, fair, glowing skin and golden curls. You know Maya could have any man she wanted because of her beauty, but then Kaif Ali is not bad either, is he? They do go well together.'

'Have I seen him?'

'Well, only you'd know that!' replied Maansi.

'Maansi, you'd know if I've been to his house.'

'None of us go to his house, and especially not since the incident. No one talks to them any more but you have probably seen him. He's the one who owns the spice shop in the bazaar. He's normally sitting on the verandah of his shop, looking at the passers-by.'

'Passers-by... people like Maya!'

'No, not really, for she hardly comes, but if it was up to her – and believe me she's a rebel and still immature and easily influenced – she probably would. She says she still loves him even though he was never really hers. She says, in love, it's not really about getting or making the love of your life part of your life – it is not necessary all the time – it is just the fact that you have loved and experienced that wonderful feeling. Two hearts beating as one, separate bodies but inseparable souls.'

'Oh Maansi, you have been watching too many movies. But what a tragic story about *mothers and daughters, a sister and a wife.*'

'I've not been watching too many movies. Maya believes that, and as for me, I don't believe in things like that, this love business. Anyway, do you feel like that? You are married and love Suhaan.'

'Love and marriage are two different things,' I answered. 'I am married, but for love I can imagine that feeling when I look at Haari. I have never felt this for Suhaan, or for anyone else either. Maansi, love and sex to you, I think, are almost the same. They have absolutely nothing to do with one another. One is love, the other is lust.'

'Like you had with Rocky...' she said, grinning cheekily.

'Well, maybe for him, yes. For me no, because I agreed so that I could get my passport. No love or lust.'

With all this talking time had flown by and Haari was fast asleep on the blanket on the floor as Maansi and I sat on either side. His face was nearly as light as mine, his hair darker than mine. His looks were so perfect and round, not like mine. I had very feminine features. He was untouched and unspoilt, but his mother was both of those things and more.

I used to wonder what life would be like if I didn't have this little bit of freedom, on my own with Maansi. We only went to the bazaar every now and again, and into the small town about every other week. Apart from that, nowhere else. I had not made India a part of my life and never asked Suhaan to take me out sightseeing, and nor did he ask if I wanted to go. Maybe that would have been a good idea as we may have bonded, and perhaps fallen in love, but who knows if you can actually love animals as your partner, for his actions even now were still the same.

'Come inside,' said Suhaan as he walked out of the gate and off to the bazaar.

'Go and see who's at the gate, child. Who is Suhaan letting in?'

'OK, Suhaani Ma. You stay asleep. I'll go and see.'

'Maya, come inside. Should I call you Auntie Maya now that I know how old you are?'

'No,' she said laughing, 'Maya's fine. Listen, Sania, I heard the man with the donkey coming so I told him to come here for I want to buy you some clothes and bangles, as I was not here at your wedding. I would have danced all night for you to liven up your wedding.'

'No, thank you, I don't need any clothes as I am not staying here long, and as for glass bangles, when Suhaan holds my arms with force, they crack and my arms and hands bleed. I have stopped wearing them,' I said. 'By the way, you're so beautiful.'

She smiled. 'I insist. Please show us the best you have, and what do you have for babies?'

Finally she chose two suits of *shalwar kameez* and a *sari* for me, with a set of twenty-four glass bangles. For Haari, she chose two suit-materials and black glass bangles. Babies wear bangles in India.

She sat watching me as she put the glass bangles on my wrist, then she asked what I meant by 'not staying here for long'. I told her the truth; I told her everything. I then asked her about her love. She smiled and sighed, and simply said that some things are just not meant to be, and sometimes people just don't want others to be happy. She then asked me if I loved Suhaan. Once again I told her truth. I don't know why, but she seemed trustworthy. She then quietly lifted her beautiful eyes up, with tears rolling down her cheeks. She held my hands tightly and pushed the bangles up over my wrists, and said calmly, 'Is that why you had an affair with Bhaskar? Do you love him?'

'What?' I started blushing. How did she know? It must have been blabbermouth Maansi. How could she?

'It's OK,' she continued, 'you can trust me. He's my brother, he tells me everything.'

'I don't love Rocky. I only agreed because I needed information and my passport. That's all. I needed help.'

'He did mention something.'

'He did, and did he help me? No. He helped himself.

Did he tell you how he raped me also? That's when it all began.'

'Tell me the whole truth, Sania.'

The tears were still rolling down her cheeks as she heard the full story of Rocky and me.

After a long while she said, 'I've got to go now, Sania. If Suhaani Ma hears me crying she'll suspect, but I guarantee you that your passport, or a new passport, you'll get. I'll get to the bottom of this if it's the last thing I do.'

Those were her final words as she left our courtyard, head held down, long curls reaching her bottom, her scarf draped on one side, head uncovered, arms swinging by her hips. Suhaani Ma was calling her name, telling her to stay and have tea as she was just about to get up to make some. She ignored the calling. I followed her and then stopped. I didn't know what to believe. How would it be possible? Was she getting my hopes up for nothing, especially as I was almost – yes, almost – getting used to the idea that this was my life and nothing else would happen? She stood at the gate, gazing from her red eyes. She waved and closed the gate behind her, never to be seen again. She was a *sister* and a *daughter*; me, a *wife* and a *mother* and no longer my parent's daughter!

Secrets Revealed and Dreams Deserted

EVERY TIME THE gate opened I imagined Maya walking into our courtyard, her black locks caressing her bosom and, at the back, a tassel of curls falling down her back. You could tell that she took care of her locks, unlike most of the women there. They oiled it every day and either plaited it neatly, or curled it around their fingers into a coiled bun. No one really let their hair loose. You could tell that their hair was long but scraggly, thin and in bad condition. One thing was certain – they never trimmed it every couple of months.

'Never to be seen again' was exactly how I felt, for a week had gone by and there was no sign of Maya, or a message from her either. Maansi was still coming. We three still went into the fields, but neither Maansi nor I had seen Maya. I knew she was a strong, rebellious character, but that didn't mean that she could work miracles. After all, she hadn't helped herself a great deal, had she?

Seconds turned into minutes, minutes into hours, hours into days, days into nights, nights full of loneliness and days full of hope, days and nights together quickly turned into another week. Saturday came, the day when I was born, the days after a whole week at school, a day when we – Papa, Mama and I – all went shopping, a day to celebrate life by enjoying it, going out. Saturdays here were the same as all the other days because, all days were the same. I could tell that this Saturday was doomed to be different by the look on Maya's face as she arrived. The only thing that came to my mind was, 'Is today going to change the rest of my life?' Somehow I didn't think so. Devastation was looming.

'Hello Maya.'

'Hello Sania.'

'How are you?'

'I'm well, Sania. How about you?'

'I'm fine. Both of you, please sit.'

Maya, Rocky and I sat on the same bed just under the lime tree, for it gave us shade and scent. All the fruit and flowers smelt wonderful because of the heat, but didn't work wonders for humans. It was a little too hot to bear. Heat for fruit is like heaven but for humans it can be like hell. Most people changed their clothes, sometimes every day, sometimes every other day, but some changed only once a week, at the same time as their bathing. Because of the extremity of the heat they and their clothes smelt of sweat most of the time.

Suhaani Ma (goodness knows why she called her son by nearly the same name as her own) was at home. She was inside, but when she saw Maya and Rocky sitting there with me, she came out and started with a polite greeting. Suhaan was tending to the goats that were in the far corner. As they bleated away he coated their heads with oil, making them gleam, while he fed them almonds. He had never attended to me like that, ever. He put his hand up to acknowledge their arrival and smiled at them as he finished off his chores.

After washing his hands, he came and shook hands with Rocky and said his greetings to Maya. Suhaani Ma had already, at this point, kissed Maya on both of her cheeks and put her hand over her head, wishing her well. She kissed Rocky on his forehead and once again put her hand over his back, wishing him a long life. *If she knew what he had been doing to me*, I thought, *I'd be out by my ear and he would have got cursed rather than praised.*

'Suhaan, when are you and Sania going to England?' asked Maya.

'We're not,' replied Suhaan.

'Why not? Don't you want to?'

'No, not really.'

'What's "not really"? Everyone wants to go to England. There isn't any other reason, is there?'

'Apart from the fact that Father is still away, that's it really.'

'Anything else?' she asked, trying to get some real answers out of him.

'No… Anyway, why are you asking? What does it have to do with you?'

'So, if your father came back then you would go, right? And you have the relevant documents, right? There's nothing to hold you back.'

'Yes,' he muttered, slowly.

As I've said before, I act on impulse a lot, and as I heard this, I instantly blurted out, 'We don't have the relevant papers, the most important ones, the passports!'

'Really, Sania? Now let's see if Suhaan can shed some light on the passports,' Maya said in a mocking tone.

'Why you asking me? I've already said, that's it.'

'Well, Suhaan, you just said you had the relevant documents and now Sania says you don't. Tell the truth, Suhaan.'

Then, in a nervous tone, and looking down, he said, quietly, 'It is.'

'It is what?'

'Shut up, noisy woman. Go and mind your own business.'

'Right, I see it's not going to work like this. Let's start again, this time, let's try Bhaskar…' Maya turned her face towards her brother and continued, 'Do you know anything about the passports?'

Before he even had a chance to reply, I quickly opened my big mouth and blurted out, 'Of course he does. That's why I used to go to him and that's—'

'Be quiet, Sania,' interrupted Maya, 'Now Bhaskar, I was talking to you.'

'I'm telling you he knows. That's why—' I was still talking.

'I beg your pardon,' Suhaan butted in. 'When did you go to Bhaskar and what happened?'

Suddenly I realised the extent of the damage I was about to cause, exposing my own secret. No wonder Maya told me to be quiet. She was trying to protect me, after all Bhaskar had nothing to lose. I paused, and then replied with a red, embarrassed face, 'Well, on the day before I got married, Bhaskar asked why I was so sad. I told him that I needed my passport as Dev had taken it. So he said he was going to see if he could find out where my passport was. That's it.'

Suhaan was no fool. He roared, 'That's not what it sounded like to me. You are lying now. Your face is red and you're embarrassed. So that's not the truth.'

Suddenly, Maya turned the attention away from me, thank God, saying, 'If that's not the truth then what is the truth, Suhaan?'

'Come on, Suhaan, what's the truth?' asked Bhaskar, as if he did not care if he wound him up, but then that was obvious because, as I have already said, he had nothing to lose.

'You shut up as well,' snapped Suhaan. 'What's my wife been coming to you for, eh? Come on, answer.'

'Well, well… you tell me and I'll tell you.'

With that Suhaan was even more furious. Suhaani Ma kept saying, 'Calm down, calm down!' He was not listening.

Suhaan went on, 'That means she did come to you, you filth… for what?'

Somehow Bhaskar was enjoying winding Suhaan up. Maya stepped in, telling him that it was nothing like what he thought. Instead he should think of what he knows.

To break the ice between Suhaan and myself I quickly suggested that he knew nothing about the passports, as he had already told me this, and he would never lie. Bhaskar then said, slyly, that he had been lying. I called him a liar but he laughed in my face. I felt so sad that he was lying. Why was he lying about my Suhaan, my husband? That is exactly what I told him. Maya stepped in again and told me to stop crying as it was making things worse.

I could tell from her tone that she was really annoyed, especially because I would not stop crying.

'For heaven's sake, Suhaan, tell her the truth.'

'Yes, all right,' he blurted out coldly.

My crying stopped and I said, 'Yes, what Suhaan? Please tell me.'

He then told me that he had had the passport since our marriage. Dev had given it to him as promised. He went on to explain that he hadn't said he did not have the passport, he just had not said yes either. So, in fact, he hadn't lied. I started crying again, and kept saying how he lied all that time, all those years. He said it was because he could not leave as his father was away, and so he didn't want my constant nagging. *Secrets revealed and my dreams deserted.*

Nagging! He didn't even know what nagging was. Then I really started nagging, telling him how he had betrayed me with his lies; how I hated him for doing so; how I had made my own mistakes because of his lies. He kept saying, 'Shut up, shut up, foolish girl,' which made me even more angry. I charged at him but he was a man and quicker at violence than I. He grabbed the griddle and in an instant he had me pinned against the wall with the griddle at my neck. He told me that if I made another sound he would beat me with the rolling pin that was next to the griddle.

Suhaani Ma charged towards him and told him to behave. Maya also tried to calm him down, telling him not to hurt me, that it was not what men are supposed to do. They are there to respect and protect their wives. As he looked around at her, my neck was still pinned by the griddle but I managed to push him with both hands, crying at the top of my voice, shouting, 'Liar, liar, you'll be cursed, liar.' With these words he became violent again, picking up his flip-flop to hit me. He put it down when his mother told him to stop. Then he went to find a stick, shouting, 'I'm going to kill her.'

I could see him search for a stick, and sure enough he found one in the wood that was kept for the fire. He came charging back. Bhaskar watched on as Maya looked closely at his footsteps. As soon as he got close to me, he swung the stick like a bat as if to clobber a ball, the ball on this occasion being me. All of a sudden, Maya grabbed him forcefully by the arm so he couldn't move any more, while she watched my tears roll down my cheeks: years full of secrets, unfelt tears, revelations, all out in the open.

In an urgent yet calm tone, Maya spoke – such true words, words of wisdom: 'Wipe away the tears, Sania, that make you and other women like you so weak. Don't bow your head to Suhaan or any other man, only to God. Certainly not to those we give birth to, nurture all our lives, feed them our bodies without hesitation, care for as sisters, caress sensually as their wives and above all, respect them as our fathers and brothers. These relationships tie us to them and each one of these relationships makes us weak because we, yes, we the females, give them the upper hand, the power, leaving ourselves to be treated as second-class citizens.'

With these words, I stopped crying. Suhaan's stick fell away to the floor and Suhaani Ma gasped in disbelief at how a woman could say all this, and especially to me. Haari, my big boy, had happily slept through all of it.

'Come on, Bhaskar, let's go.' Maya turned to Suhaan, 'And, oh yes, Suhaan, give the passport to her and let her decide what she wants to do, not you. If you don't, I'll be back and I'll make sure that I get it for her, so better you do it yourself.'

Then they both left. This was the first time that Suhaani Ma had not asked her guests to stay and sit a while longer. As they went to close the gate behind them, Maya pointed a finger at Suhaan, a gentle reminder of what she had ordered.

From all this the only regret, or lucky escape, that I had was that, thank goodness, my affair with Bhaskar remained undisclosed, no thanks to me, as Bhaskar and I had nearly given the game away. Now that Maya had set the ball rolling and the truth was finally out, I knew I couldn't let it rest! Suhaan went off into the bazaar to play cards with his friends. Suhaani Ma went inside, put her fan on high and lay on the bed resting and thinking. She was not asleep and she left the door open just in case there were any more dramas. I carried on with my normal chores of the day. In the evening I kept myself to myself, trying to avoid any confrontation or eye contact.

A few days had gone by and things were back to normal. I thought it would be good to bring up the subject of my passport, just a gentle reminder really. I simply asked Suhaan when I was going to get my passport. Also, how would I be able to take Haari, and what about his passport and his rights to go with me as my husband to the UK. He remained silent and I just thought that he might not be fully awake yet, as it was still only breakfast time. I started repeating my words, when suddenly he snapped, shouting that he did not want to hear rubbish any more. I was about to say something in my defence when he put his face up to mine, put his finger on his lips and said, 'No more, shhh... silence.' The demon inside of me awakened. I really don't know why I was so angry. I wasn't that angry when he was throttling me with the griddle or when he started to come towards me with the stick to beat me to a pulp. Maybe it was because, deep down inside, I knew that this was my last chance of escaping the country – after all, that was all I wanted.

I had to plan my action all by myself, and carefully as well. The timing had to be right because it had to be done when it was siesta time. That was the only time that no one went to anyone else's house, or hardly ever anyway. I had planned it for the very next day, a Saturday, a good day, but then I postponed because I did not want the day to be tainted by ill feelings. It was a good day for me. My plan was put to the extreme on a Sunday instead.

We had just had lunch, a serving of rice and lentils, no salad, no fruit, but plenty of water. I washed the dishes and tidied everything away. I asked Suhaan to sharpen the knife for me. He asked me why, as I was always cutting myself. I told him I needed to slaughter someone. He laughed, saying that it must be him. I said no, and then he said that we didn't have any meat and left it at that. He did, however, sharpen the knife for me. Suhaani Ma went for her daily nap at two o'clock and I picked up Haari who was fast asleep. I sat on the small bench near the man-made stove, picked up the knife and woke Haari. He was so tired that he started to cry. The more I shook him, the more he cried.

Soon Suhaan came from the garden and said, 'Why aren't you quietening him down?'

In a rage I answered back, 'This time I am going to make him quiet for ever, watch.'

He watched me, puffing and panting and in a real rage, holding Haari, not really hurting him but making as if I was. He was crying because he was tired and that was the plan. I made it look as if he were crying because I was hurting him. I took the knife and, as Suhaan watched, I took it to his neck and then I started crying and laughing hysterically, shouting that I would slit his throat and my own. I kept saying how he was going to join Kez very soon.

As he stepped forward, I said that if he came any closer I would definitely end his child's life quicker. I then repeated his words, 'No more, shhh... silence. While I just make a tiny incision and then make mincemeat out of it.'

At that point he seemed to start hallucinating, especially as I carried on saying that I'd feed the heart to the goats, the liver would be good for the cow, the kidneys good for us humans as ours pack up early so we'd eat them. He screamed and called his mother, shouting her name, 'Suhaani Ma, Suhaani Ma, my only child...'

She came out in a daze because she had been woken from her sleep. She gasped for breath when she saw what Suhaan saw. She started to cry as well. This day, for the first time, they both looked helpless, and even though I felt really bad for doing it, in a perverse kind of way I had the upper hand. Suhaani Ma kept saying, 'Why, why child?'

I told her that Suhaan had to make a decision: Haari and me dead, or England. I also told her that because of her, the old bat, Suhaan would not leave. I said that mothers-in-law like her have often ended up being burnt alive. You could say that whatever came into my head I blurted out. I knew it was not nice, and most definitely wrong.

I don't know how or what exactly turned their decision around, but whatever it was, it worked. They both promised that they would tell Suhaan's father and then when he came, or was going to come, all three would leave together. Suhaan said he would come with me to the embassy and get the relevant papers that would enable us all to leave India for England. I said that if they broke their promise then I would do whatever and they wouldn't even know. They'd only know when it was too late! They promised that on the following day it would be a new beginning, and sure enough it was. I felt really bad for using Haari as a pawn to get what I wanted but I had no choice.

The next day lived up to its promises. I was almost as if I could smell the coffee of the UK's cafés, and the scones and clotted cream of the Yorkshire tea rooms, and of course the fresh smell of hot bread being baked. Oh, how wonderful. I was so happy that every time I went to the embassy I stopped for a coffee to live out my future.

Suhaan and I were not close, but we were not strangers after this incident. I started being a lot nicer as I saw my time getting nearer and nearer – like seeing the light at the end of the tunnel. The tunnel was not scary any more. There was a ray of hope in it, always.

Maya came a few weeks later and I told her the good news without telling her what I had done. She wept tears of joy and all I could say was thank you. She asked if Maansi had come and it was then that I realised that, because of my own troubles, I had forgotten that she had not come in a long time. I asked Maya if she knew why she hadn't come. She replied that it was nothing. I knew that was a lie.

The following day had a bad smell about it as normally it rained a lot in the monsoon season, and when it rains, most of the time, it does so in the night, so first thing in the morning there was a beautiful, fresh, clean, crisp smell in the air, but today it was musky with a mouldy damp smell. After breakfast I took Haari and went to see Maansi. She was not chatting or playing around. Instead she was inside, cleaning. I went to talk to her but she was not in a mood to talk. I could tell that she had been crying.

I knew that no one in that house would tell me so I went off to Auntie Khushi who would explain. Maansi was married as a child to a man who was, at that time, fifty years of age, and would now have been in his sixties. He had gone off to England and promised to come back when she was old enough to be married, about sixteen. They would then have a proper ceremony and live as man and wife. He never came back as he felt ashamed that he was older than a father figure, so how could he marry her? He never married anyone else but obviously felt it was not right to marry Maansi either. He never told them this, so they waited. Now it was too late. He had died and his body was being brought back to India to lay to rest for ever.

She went on to say that Maansi would never ever wed. She was a widow for life. I asked how that would be possible as she was only a child. She explained that in a small village like theirs culture can be bent to suit individuals, and so Maansi would dress in plain clothes and live life like a widow. I told Auntie Khushi that Maansi had said to me that her Rajah, the man of her dreams, would come one day on his white horse and take his bride away with him. She said yes because she knew he lived far away.

I felt so sorry for Maansi but what could I do for her? I went to see her many times again, but there was no change really. We never went out or chatted for a long time. We talked very little about life but she never talked about hers. But then how could she? She'd had a lifetime of dreams, all now vanished; her dreams had deserted her, never to come true, ever.

Our tickets had come and we were ready to leave the village in a couple of days' time. Those couple of days I tried to spend with Maansi, but still there was no glimpse of joy in her eyes at all. The evening before our departure I went to see her for the last time. I told her I would write and tele- phone, but she requested that I didn't, otherwise I too would be hurt because she wouldn't come to the phone, and would not reply to my letters. As I let go of her hand she slowly uttered, 'I wish I could have been in your place. You're so lucky.'

I suppose, compared to her, I was. I gave her a smile as she waved. She showed no joy at our friendship because she was disheartened with life. She knew this was to be the rest of her life. My heart really ached for her but I could not do a thing.

I left a whole case of goodies for Maansi and a few letters so that when she felt better she could read them. I also left her my address so that she could write, but knew that it was not going to happen in the near future. I asked Suhaani Ma for forgiveness and she was happy to oblige. She was a woman. Was it that women find it easier to forgive, or the other way around? She blessed us both and hugged Haari quite a few times in our final days. She said she was not worried as her husband was coming in a few days. She then smiled and told me that they had known this before my drama! No wonder they said yes. I had done all that drama for nothing! She smiled, a smile of wisdom; me, still very much a child.

Dire Consequences

AS THE AEROPLANE door opened the warm air hit my face. It was so calming because I had got used to the scorching temperatures but had not liked. This warm air felt so good. I could tell that it was about the mid-twenties Celsius. Suhaan and Haari were looking a bit puzzled as to this new environment, and why shouldn't they? This was not their home – a place that they knew nothing about, an alien environment. But then I had been an alien living in an alienating environment for years. I felt like saying to Suhaan, 'Now it's your turn!' but I didn't.

I was carrying Haari in my arms as he would not walk, and of course Suhaan would not carry him as he felt that it was not a manly thing to do. This nurturing business was for women. I was carrying him on the front, on my stomach, but climbing down the stairs was getting difficult, so I swapped him onto my hip on my right side. He hung around my neck and with his left hand he slipped his two fingers down into the waist folds of my sari. That was his comfort zone, either his fingers on my skin on the back or into my bust area.

I knew that the answer would be no to carrying Haari, but still I asked Suhaan if he would carry Haari or the two bags we had as hand luggage. With my child on the right side, bag on the left shoulder and one in his left hand, we strode into Heathrow Airport. I chatted politely to the staff there while they checked our documents. I went straight through but then went back to Suhaan's queue as he was not a British citizen. He was asked some questions but he could not understand a word. They then asked me to wait outside while they interviewed him with an interpreter. They then called me in and I wrote down the details of where we would be staying. They said they would be in touch, and in a year, if all goes well, he would get his residency rights to remain indefinitely in the UK. I got the luggage trolley and we all waited for our baggage. It had already come, it seemed, a long time ago, as one of the cases was on the floor, rather than on the belt. I put the luggage on the trolley, along with Haari, and pushed my way out to where we were being met.

In the distance I could see her ginger hair as it was so striking. As we got close she started shouting, 'Here, here!' I could not help but smile. It was Charlie. We embraced each other with hugs and kisses and tears of joy as well. I then introduced her to Suhaan and looked on as they shook hands. She then smiled and kissed Haari, saying how cute he was. I thanked her for coming as the journey to the airport was over three hours. She said she would not have missed it for anything in the world; this from the woman who was old enough to be my mother and yet was young at heart like me.

Suhaan, Haari and I sat in the back as Charlie drove like a maniac, as usual. Papa used to say to her that one day she would be responsible for her own death. She would always reply that there was no need to hide or fear death as it would come when it was meant to. It was not the quantity of life but the quality. Throughout the journey I talked to Charlie in English, of course, and tried to explain some bits to Suhaan in Hindi as well, even though he was too tired, and too furious as well for being left out. Haari was calm and sleepy and felt at ease in my arms. Every time she said she could not believe how thin I had become, he became even more furious. However, he did not say anything.

Our journey flew by as we drove up to our road. I remembered how Papa used to drive up with me watching out for him. This time I knew that no one would be watching out for me, and sure enough I was right. It was still light outside as it was only seven o'clock, just in time for dinner. But today there would be no Mama, so no dinner waiting either. Charlie went to open the front door. I quickly told her that I wanted to open it myself. I had my set of keys still in my handbag. I opened the door. There was no aroma of incense, just a lonesome place where no one tread any more. No smell of anyone. The house was exactly the way we had left it, clean, neat and tidy. Charlie had kept it that way.

I took Haari and sat on the sofa for a long, long time, without uttering a word, thinking back to the days of my father's death; the aftermath of it all and then to the days of us leaving. *Well,* I thought, *at least no one from school was going to come asking me to go back.* I was now old enough to decide. So many of my years has slipped by.

Suhaan lay on the sofa beside where I was sitting, while Charlie put the luggage upstairs. She then brought some food that she had in the kitchen for us, some tea and snacks. We all ate on the sofa rather than the dining table, and then she left as she knew we were all exhausted. I went into my bedroom but my luggage was not there. I knew she had taken the bags into the big bedroom because now there were three of us. There was no way that I could sleep on my mama and papa's bed, no way. I dragged the cases into my old room by which time Suhaan was snoring away. I got Haari, gave him the bottle that Charlie kindly made before leaving, and dozed off myself without even changing my clothes or his.

Very early in the morning the sun had shone straight through the window as I had not remembered to draw the curtains. I tossed and turned but Haari was still so fast asleep in between us both. I looked at my clock. It was barely 6 a.m. I could not sleep any more. I looked around the room with all my past in it. It was as if I had just woken up from a bad dream. I then felt the warmth of my son and, with the constant reminder of Suhaan's snoring, I knew it was reality. Time had not stood still and neither had I. I had lived a life too, a life full of stories to tell. I lay there thinking about my future and knew that, finally, it was in my own hands. What was I going to decide for us three? I had to, as a woman, a second-class citizen in India, hold this family together for this was the only one I had. No matter what, I had to make it work.

Life was pretty normal. The local boys had all gone off to college or work, and when we did meet they were mature about my circumstances. Suhaan was adamant that I should not speak to other men as I was a married woman. One thing was for sure: I never went out to play football any more, even though a few of them still did. Charlie was there, always helpful, but on the whole I tried to manage without her.

I signed on at the local social security office and told them I needed money to survive as I had a husband who, legally, could not work due to not yet having his permanent residency. I got my dole money and it was enough for the basics. I asked Suhaan to find a job at the local shops, after all he could only do basic work due to his lack of English. There were Asian corner shops but he refused to do demeaning jobs, as he called them, like cleaning and stacking shelves. He only wanted to operate the till and help customers. No one gave him a job and no one was surprised either, as he didn't want to start at the bottom.

My nineteenth birthday had come and gone and only Charlie remembered. She came with love, a present, a card and a small cake. Charlie asked Suhaan why and how he forgot my birthday. In reply he told her that birthdays are not important, especially not grown ups; maybe a child, yes.

He had picked up a few English words with his Asian friends whom he hung around with around the shops. They talked, smoked and drank. He started to go out with them every day and that was his normal routine. One day, when he came home, I asked why he had said that to Charlie about my birthday. He replied he had said it because it was the truth. I then asked him why was it when Haari had turned one in India we hadn't celebrated the birthday then. He replied saying Haari was too young to know about birthdays. To some extent it was true, I suppose.

It was Christmas time again and I was spending quite a lot of time with Charlie, especially because Suhaan was out a lot, although not as much as before because of the shortened days. When he got home around seven I had to be home, that was the rule, and the few times I wasn't he was furious. At Christmas he didn't want to go to Charlie's parties but I did. We fought long and hard, him saying that we were not Christians, so we didn't celebrate Christmas. I reminded him that, in fact, I was half Christian. He always felt humiliated whenever I told him that. He always said that it was a disgrace what my mother did, marrying an Englishman. Going against his wishes, I went to Charlie's party, and because he wouldn't look after Haari, I took him with me. The night was young and we were all sitting in the lounge talking, Haari in my lap. It was about eight o'clock when the doorbell rang. Charlie went to open the door. I could hear Suhaan at the door asking for me. Charlie told him to come inside. He refused. She asked him again but he still refused. Finally I got up and left Haari on the sofa.

'Hi, Suhaan, come in,' I said.

'Get home now.'

'No, Suhaan. I've cooked your food. You can eat it or you can come in. Otherwise I will be back in about an hour.'

'If you know what's good for you, you'll come now,' he threatened.

'Now? Because you say so? I can decide for myself, you know.'

'I've said it, haven't I?'

'Tough luck, but now I do what I want. I'm free and I'm not going to be dominated by you any more.'

'Perhaps you'd better go, Sani?' said Charlie, looking a bit embarrassed.

'No, I'm staying. *He* comes home when he likes, why not me?'

With that he looked even more furious, even though it was not so noticeable on his skin, but from his nod, the slight nod, the kind of nod that the famous actor, hunk and romantic lover of Suhaan's heyday, Rajesh Khanna, used to give when disappointed. Rajesh was the hero in the seventies in the Bollywood film industry, the heart of Indian cinema. But Suhaan was not a hero, not even in the eyes of his wife. Neither was he a hunk or a romantic lover.

At nine o'clock, as promised, I left Charlie's and went home to face the music. I opened the door and went straight upstairs to put Haari to bed as he was already fast asleep and it was past his bedtime. It only took a few minutes as I just took off his top and bottoms so he could sleep in his vest and pants, as he always did. He was already out of nappies because in India there were hardly any in the village, so Haari grew up doing his business on the floor wherever and whenever.

As I came downstairs I remembered the bend in the stairs, and how this was my safe haven on the awful night when my father died. I asked Suhaan if he wanted to eat or drink anything as I walked towards him. He ignored me. I didn't bother asking anything else and I could see the dirty plates on the coffee table in front of the television. As I sat down next to him he got up and told me to stand as well. I refused. He stood looking at me angrily, shouting about how I had made a fool of him. I refused to reply to any of his angry remarks.

In a split second he threw the plates off the coffee table, and then threw the table over, ranting and raving. He went towards the television and bent his leg as if to kick it.

'Don't you dare,' I shouted, 'this is not yours, so you have no right!'

With this comment he charged towards me, not to hit or kick me, but to strip my clothes off me instead. He was hysterical, pulling and tugging at my clothes. Suddenly he pulled my skirt so hard that it tore away at the zip. He had me in his clutches. He pulled at my blouse, which did not need much tugging as the buttons just flew open. I felt humiliated as I stood there with a torn skirt and my blouse fully open with my underwear showing. He grabbed my waist-length, long, straight hair and twirled it around my neck, tightening his grip all the while, pulling and keeping the noose as tight as possible. I was yelling in anger, but then I should have been used to it as he had done this so many times in India. It was a way of controlling, dominating and intimidating me.

The more I tried to break free, the tighter the noose around my neck became, and then he reinforced this by clasping my neck with his arm as well. Suddenly I became silent because I could hear Haari crying. It was not like him to wake up but with all the noise he was obviously disturbed. I begged Suhaan to let me go and pleaded with him to think of Haari. He replied by saying that now I knew who was actually in control – him. I had to promise that I would do as he asked and then he would let me go. I ran upstairs, scared in my own home, in my own environment, fearing for myself and for my child. Was this the life that I wanted for my child?

Slowly and reluctantly I came back downstairs. He was still waiting in the same position to finish what he had started. I sat down and carried on soothing Haari, but he would not settle easily. I put him on the sofa and tapped him in a rocking motion. He started to doze off. As Suhaan saw Haari drift off to sleep he slowly grabbed me by the hair and forced me up. As I stood up my eyes were tilting down, and he knew that I was crying, silently. He then asked why I didn't do as he asked. I replied that I had not done anything wrong. He then said that 'wrong' was not what he had asked and that I needed to be taught a lesson.

As before, he pulled and ripped at my clothes as I tried to break free, but he had my hair, the 'enchanting darkness' as he had called it. The tears were still rolling. He was trying to rip every bit of my clothing off, including my underwear.

'Please, Suhaan, don't do this. Please don't force yourself on me, especially in front of Haari. He may wake up, please. It is humiliating to do this in front of a child and... and so shameful for us. Have a heart.'

All my begging and pleading fell on deaf ears as he took no notice. I felt so belittled and wondered if God were listening to me or watching, what He would do and why He wasn't controlling the situation. Why wasn't He stopping Suhaan? Was God a man? Why was it that women are made to feel inferior to men? Why was it that God had given men more strength than women, why? If women were born stronger than men, would they have done the same things to men? Would they dominate men in the same way?

I was screaming now, hysterical, suggesting that we go upstairs, to be away from Haari, to do what he wanted to, but he would not listen to any pleading. He was now busy performing his disgraceful act when suddenly Haari woke with all the noise, the screaming, the shouting, and a lot of pulling and tugging. He stood there looking at us both. I became silent and felt disgusted that he was witnessing this. Suhaan was aware of Haari looking on and yet he felt no remorse. He didn't stop what he was doing. We were both in awkward positions, my clothes torn off and his top half covered. I was lifeless yet rigid with fright. Haari could not have known what was going on so just sat, dazed at what he could see. I stood there semi-nude.

A couple of minutes later, when Suhaan had finished with me, I grabbed Haari and rushed off upstairs to soothe him. I wrapped my gown around myself while the stream of Suhaan's lust ran down my legs. Somehow my tears just would not stop and yet there was no noise from my mouth. How could a father commit such things in front of his child? Surely these intimate things are supposed to be behind closed doors? Definitely not in front of minors. Personal things between adults are supposed to be between two people, not three. Could I allow this to carry on? Could I afford to be in this position again? More to the point, could I let Haari witness these scenes again? It was not as bad when he was a baby, but even that was unforgivable. Now it was simply unacceptable. Would he have to witness these adult scenes throughout his growing life? Actions like these always had *dire consequences*.

I went off to sleep with sore eyes from all the crying. The next day was as normal as it could be, I suppose. Suhaan went out with his friends after lunch. He had had his favourite breakfast – I made *parathas* stuffed with mince and vegetable with yoghurt on the side. He had cooked milky tea with spices. He played with Haari until lunchtime. For lunch I made him his favourite dish ever: lamb Balti-style with chapattis. I even made a dessert, as he loved his puddings. This was semolina with all the nuts he loved. He was quiet and so was I. He then asked why I had made all his favourites in one day. I didn't reply. He was full, and smiled like a lion that had just eaten his prey.

As he neared the front door I, for the first time, went to him, kissed him on the cheek and waved him goodbye. His smile got even bigger, his head held high and full of pride. Little did he know that that might be for the last time.

The house phone kept ringing so I took it off its hook. With my body motionless I put my key into the lock so he could not put his key in to open the door. Instead of pleading, which I had expected, he was roaring like thunder, telling me to open the door otherwise he was going to break my legs, or show me his manhood again. I told him only one thing: that it was because of his manhood that we were in this state today, so pick up your bag from outside the door and never return.

He wouldn't take my words seriously and kept banging. Soon the police were outside. I opened the door and told them what he had done and in return all I wanted was for him to leave and stay away. He kept saying he was going to pay me back but promised the police that he would leave me alone. After twenty minutes they all left and so the neighbours left their front gardens and went back inside, Charlie included. I did phone Charlie straight away and explained what was going on. She was shocked at why I had, and still did, put up with all this. The answer was simple: I was an Indian mother's daughter trying to keep my parents' and my own respect intact.

Strange as it may seem, the suffocation did not ease, even though Suhaan was no longer living with us. This life had its hallmarks stamped upon it; his presence was invisible but everywhere I looked I could feel him, sense and smell him. He was running through my veins, a feeling I had to accept.

Final Farewell, My Love

BRITISH SUMMERTIME HAD come and days had got longer, and so did the warm sunshine. I was going out a lot more, and enjoying life a bit more after the hibernation through the winter months, but life was still not good. Why and how, I could not put my finger on.

Suhaan had phoned many times pleading for me to sign his 'right to stay' documents so that he could become a British citizen. I didn't want to send him back as he would feel humiliated in front of his parents, especially now because his father had returned from Germany to stay with his family. Suhaan was now the sole provider.

A couple of days before my birthday a knock on my door changed my fate; a decision I had made had been reversed. The officials from the Home Office needed proof that he was actually living with me. I could have lied as some of his clothes were still in the house, but instead I chose to tell the truth. They spelt out their conclusion carefully: not husband and wife, Suhaan couldn't stay. He would be escorted back home within a month. His year was already up and they had already shown a lot of compassion.

The choice was mine to make once again. The immigration police had come and taken him late one evening while he was playing cards with his friends, the ones he was staying with. He looked at me in disgrace as they escorted him. He turned his head back to get a last glimpse at his son. His son would be his for ever, but not his wife. I was not his wife legally anyway as we never did register our marriage, but morally we were man and wife in the eyes of the Lord, not in the eyes of the law. The aeroplane would be waiting miles and miles away, his seat would have his name on it. He would see London only for a short while. His next vision would be the heated tarmac of his own home. His tears rolled down silently as he asked me to hear his cries: 'Hear me cry... hear my cries.' I did exactly that, but it was all an illusion; a bad dream. The reality was what I made it.

On my birthday he came knocking at the door offering, for the very first time, flowers, a card and a packet of plums, or so he thought, as it was actually beetroot. I opened the door, asked him in and told him the reality. He agreed to behave and sleep in the other bedroom. He said he had learnt his lesson and was sorry and would behave. He kept his promise and within a few weeks we had our registry office wedding as proof for the official papers. Officials still came on a few occasions to check that he was indeed living with me. Everyone was satisfied, including Suhaan.

Now that he was living with me again I prayed that he had changed his behaviour over the last few months. He promised that this was the new man and the old Suhaan was no more. Even though he had been so bad towards me, something deep down inside me wanted him to stay, and an aching feeling embedded in my heart pondered relentlessly into wanting him to stay for ever; for him to make me his the way it should be, the way they show it in films. I wanted to be loved, to be cared for, to be respected, not worshipped and most certainly not lusted after, for that's how it had been all this time.

Time, they say, is a great healer, and even though I could never forget, I did begin to forgive him. We actually started to sit and talk like normal couples. We talked about our past, the brighter future, our child and the many more he wanted. We talked about photographs, or rather the lack of them, as we had none of the two of us, or with Haari. We laughed about how it was a difficult time for us all and yet I still had bought a birthday cake for myself. Every year I can remember having a cake, maybe not even all the years spent in India. The cakes there did not taste the same as they were made with products that were one hundred per cent natural, so tasted very rich compared to the ones in England that have artificial colours, additives and preservatives. The cake has always been a symbol of celebration, which is why we didn't have it on my wedding or my mama's in India.

Charlie had also been present on all my birthdays that took place in England, and on this birthday she was the bearer of good news. Was this the reason for my good mood and leniency and a reason for my kind nature to shine through, rethinking my future and that of my child?

The cake had made me realise just how much I really missed my mama, even now, as she used to make my cake with love, all by herself, with pride. I could see this year's cake becoming a thing of the past, and next year it would be replaced by one that was handmade with pride. Charlie had become a symbol of all my birthdays in England and this year, after giving me my present, she told me how someone had told her that they had seen my mama. Charlie did not believe them, so they gave her a telephone number where Mama could be reached.

Christmas time had come again, bringing back the awful memory of last year, but this year Suhaan and I were still in the same house, my house, Papa and Mama's house. He was still sleeping in the other bedroom. Not on their bed, I made that very clear, but on the cabin bed which was always under the big window for when I couldn't sleep in my own room as a child. I would always creep in and sleep there, and then make an excuse of a bad dream. I used to move in between them both. In the four months Suhaan had turned over a new leaf, we had not become husband and wife, but had definitely become friends who actually got on with one another, surprisingly.

Suhaan said calmly one evening, while watching television, that I should go to Charlie's Christmas party. I replied by saying that I couldn't afford to have a repeat performance of last year, so would not be going. He then surprised me by saying that, if it helped me, he would come also. Well, that really did surprise me. I felt convinced that he was a changed man. I had believed that a leopard could never change its spots but somehow, in his own subtle way, he was proving me wrong!

My confidence and trust in him grew stronger and stronger, and it was then that I confided in him for the first time about what Charlie had told me about Mama on my birthday. It was not a shock to him but was surprised that I kept it to myself all this time as he said that she had to be alive and couldn't disappear into thin air. He told me to phone her once I told him I had her number. But, I told him, she knew our number and, really, as the mother, someone who was still responsible for me, she should phone me. He said I should not be petty and should make the first move to finding Mama. So I dialled the number. The receiver was picked up.

'Hello? Hello? Hello?' I repeated down the phone. Silence. 'Hello… is anyone there? I know someone's there because you've picked up the phone. Please speak, please. I want to talk to Radika, Radika Craven, Doctor Craven's wife, my mama, Sania Hema Craven's mother… please… please.'

Still there was silence.

'I knew there would be no point phoning,' I said to Suhaan. 'After all, if she wanted to talk to me she would have phoned. It's almost as if she's watching me silently, aware of everything I do but keeping a distance between me and her. But why? It doesn't make sense at all.'

'No, that's not true, Sania,' said Suhaan. 'If it was your mother on the end of the line she would've answered, be sure of that. It must be a wrong number.'

I could feel my facing burning with anxiety and also embarrassment. Why wouldn't she speak? Didn't she want her Sania any more? Didn't she love me any more?

'Throw that number away,' Suhaan continued, 'otherwise it will eat away at you every time you see it. Forget about it.'

'That's what I was trying to do, but no, you insisted that I phone and humiliate myself into knowing that my mother does not want me any more. Are you happy now?'

With that I could not control the tears flowing from my eyes, even though I didn't really want to cry for her as she didn't care. Why should I care? But, as they say, you can control your head but not your heart. There was hardly any sound of my crying except for the quiet snuffling of my nose. No one comforted me, not Suhaan, not Mama. Papa would have if he had been given the chance. Instead I cradled Haari in my arms as he held tightly to Cookie – yes, Cookie, my faithful friend – in his arms. Mother and child looked into each other's eyes, Haari motionless, his mother full of emotions, sobbing like a child, a deserted child who wanted no one, not even Suhaan for he only wanted to use me.

He sat there looking at the television. I sat looking at him. Haari sat looking at me while Cookie faced him. Angrily I tried the number again. There was silence again and yet someone picked up. The evening went by, as did many other nights, along with Christmas and New Year. Days and nights of disappointment, anger and feeling rejected. All three of us did go to Charlie's Christmas party and, to some extent, enjoyed it as well. We all came back together at ten o'clock, which was of course slightly later than the previous year. It was a fun-packed time compared to last year. Suhaan drank a little. So did I, and Haari had juice, of course.

The winter months went by so slowly and the weather and our moods, or rather my mood, was equally dreary. It was not that I was in a bad mood, more a quiet one. Staying quiet meant that I was doing a lot more thinking – silent reflections about two main aspects of my life. The first was a puzzle and amazement as to why Suhaan was being reasonable, and never forced himself on me throughout these six months. Never forced me to comply with what he wanted. The second thought was obviously about my mother.

March approached and soon the days were getting slightly longer and warmer. You could say that I had a longer day to reflect on my thoughts, but somehow the warmth made things and the thoughts seem less painful. However, this pain returned with the arrival of an invitation to my cousin's wedding. When I told Charlie about the invite she said that if my mother was alive she would definitely be there because there is no way she would not attend. She would have definitely been invited for it was her side of the family who was getting married, and she was very much family orientated. I remember when we were a family, even though Papa did not want to go to family events, Mother never missed them whether his side or her side.

Charlie and Suhaan both decided that this was an unmissable opportunity and we all had to go. So that's what we did, including Charlie. On 14 April 1986 we three sat in Charlie's car while she drove, and we made the journey from home to Bradford. We arrived at the house and as we entered, my eyes explored the numerous guests. I remembered my manners and hugged and kissed everyone that I knew, and introduced my husband, my son and my friend Charlie, who had no invite. She was made very welcome. The wedding ceremony was full of energy as there was singing, dancing, eating and lots and lots of drinking. Our journey was only a couple of hours long but Haari was tired.

This was the perfect time to check out the house to see if Mother was there.

I went from one room to another, including the bathroom. I had already checked the sitting room and the garden, but I could not see her anywhere. My heart would not accept what my eyes did not see. I wanted to see her so desperately, so, so desperately. It was as if I could smell her presence. I had already asked Nainee, the bride, and she had said no. I asked her father, Uncle Zaki, and her mother, Auntie Rubi, but all said no. Still, I was not convinced. I could sense her presence. I could smell her bodily smell, but I could not hear her laughter or her sensual voice, the depth of serenity contained within her words. There was no proof, no clue, except for my own foolish convictions.

With the flowing of free drinks Charlie was happily entertained by a toy boy and they spent most of the time flirting with one another. Why is it that Asians always find whites or fair-skinned people attractive, more so than people who look like them? It is probably because they are out of reach for them. After all, they have to marry within their own race, culture, religion or family.

Suhaan sat and talked to whoever came and sat with him. He did not move from his seat. As Haari went off to sleep I quickly went towards the bathroom, this time to use the lavatory. Suddenly someone brushed past me and then sidled away. I went into the bathroom, and then it came to me. I hurriedly opened the door and shouted, 'Mama! My mama!' I stood in frenzy, but as if my feet were frozen and my whole body lifeless. Still the fury within was ignited. The woman who had brushed past me stopped for two seconds and then quickened her pace. I ran after her, now silent. She blended into the crowd of over fifty people, three-quarters of them sober and the remainder unaware of their own existence.

I quickly found Charlie and told her. She ran around, looking everywhere. She came back and told me that I must have made a mistake. She then said that the way I had described Dev there'd be no way he would have let her come by herself, and he was nowhere to be seen. I kept telling her that, though I couldn't see the woman's face, it was strange because as she came out she covered all her face. Why, and from who? As she brushed past me, I noticed out of the corner of my eye, she had turned her face away.

I smelt her, and that lingering smell went with me into the bathroom, and it was then that my senses really awakened and I realised. I told Charlie that when I called out, she had stopped. She must have felt something. If it was not her, why would she have stopped? If it was not her why didn't she turn around, and why did she run away? The one thing for certain was that long, waist-length hair, draped as always down past her naked waist, meant it was her. It had to be her!

Charlie went and got Suhaan who just laughed in my face in disbelief. Charlie was sympathetic, but he just mocked. No matter what, I knew it was Mother. I went back upstairs and lay with Haari. He was fast asleep, and by now I was crying. No one heard as there was too much noise, and anyway, no one cared really. They say you can choose your friends but not your relatives and that blood is thicker than water. That's why I was invited. It's strange how we only met most of our very limited family members at births, deaths and weddings. We never met for the sake of it, ever. What does that say about our extended family and us? They resented Mother because she married outside of the family and hated my papa because he was English. Yet they still, for the sake of family, did what was expected of them.

My crying was not tame at all and as the tears ran down my nose, onto my cheeks and straight into my hair, I could sense my mascara running. I heard a soft footstep and then the door opening a little wider. I lifted my head up and looked at the door that was now slowly being shut. I shouted, 'Mama! Mama!' I got off the bed and opened the door. I was now silent and afraid of the unseen, afraid of the mystery. Suddenly Haari started crying. I wanted to go and find her but I couldn't leave Haari either. After all, he had no one else and I couldn't do to him what she had done to me, or could I?

I quickly grabbed him and made my way down the stairs, all the while trying to get a glimpse of her; her hair, exactly the same as it used to be and exactly the same as mine was now. If we had put our backs to one another, our hair could have been mistaken for one person's, rather than from two heads. We were both the same height, the same build, the same looks. I was still silent, but then, as I saw Charlie, the tears came again. I started shouting to her, calling her name and Suhaan's as well. She came, and I kept calling Suhaan. Finally he came. I told them both what had happened this time. Charlie remained quiet but Suhaan just shook his head and tutted in disapproval. I kept shouting, trying to prove my case, prove the truth. He raised his voice, telling me to shut up as everyone was now looking at us. He told me to stop the crying as my make-up had made me look like a clown, and to stop showing us up. I didn't care. He told me to think of my respect and his, but I ignored him, all the while crying and hugging my child tightly, the way I craved to be hugged by her.

Suhaan then said to Uncle Zaki that we had to go as our journey was long and the wedding was nearing the end. He thanked Zaki and in return Uncle Zaki thanked him for coming. Uncle Zaki asked why I was crying so much. I told him that I had seen Mama. Suhaan replied that I was mad. Both he and Uncle Zaki laughed, seemingly in a male chauvinist way. A hysterical madwoman, that's what I was! He grabbed me by my hand and pulled me towards the front door where he told Charlie that we had to leave. He dragged me in the car even though I was pleading with him that I needed to say farewell.

Our journey back home was long and dark, reflecting our moods and the environment outside. We all stayed silent and the only noise we could hear was the car engine. This bright orange car made enough noise for all of us; it was big and loud, just like Charlie. As we got out of the car she asked if I was all right, and if I wanted her to come in. I told her no, that I would be fine.

I went inside and headed off upstairs to put Haari to sleep in our bed, after all that was his bed also. It was his only bed and my bed from as far back as I can remember. I had only gone halfway up when Suhaan shouted, 'Come here.' I replied saying I would be there in a minute. His rely was, 'Now!' I ignored him but it was too late, for I had paused there and I should have gone back. Instead, I had gone up one more step. I could sense him right behind me. He grabbed my hair at the bottom and pulled it tightly. I could not move further up the stairs. Instead the pulling made me come back down the stairs in reverse, still carrying Haari in my arms. My high heels made it an impossible task but I managed it without falling backwards.

As I pleaded with Suhaan to at least let me put Haari to bed and then we could talk all he liked, he wouldn't listen. All he kept saying was that I had made us all look like fools. In one go I had shown disrespect, and made a spectacle of us all, as a family. He said that never again would he ever go to a family do and wanted to hear answers as to why I had made up this drama. Was it deliberately to pay him back for what he had done?

Whatever reply I gave him, he kept saying it was not the right answer. But if I didn't reply he got angry because I would be ignoring him. I apologised but still insisted that it was Mama I had seen, which made him even angrier. Finally I snapped and asked him exactly what he wanted. He shouted back, 'Do I need to tell you? You're an adult, you should know yourself. I don't tell you how and when to eat, do I?'

I did not have the answers to this mind game he was playing.

I faced him as I felt really uncomfortable with my hair in his clutches around my neck. I put my knee up a little, and with all my might, even though it was really difficult as I was restrained, I pushed my knee into his crotch. He bent down because of the discomfort rather than pain and so the grip on my hair loosened. I tried to move away but he was too quick for me. He pulled me by the hair so fast that Haari fell out of my arms and onto the floor. Suhaan was fuming with anger.

Throughout my life I think that I was angrier that day than ever before: Haari had fallen on the floor. He could have been hurt, but luckily escaped without any harm. He quickly got up off the floor and while crying called out, 'Mama.' I told Suhaan to let go of me but he was still infuriated by what I had done to him. All he kept saying was how dare I hit him as he had never dared hit me even though it was quite acceptable for men to hit their wives. Well, in our household it wasn't!

This comment of his made me feel so sad, to suggest that it was fine for men to hit their wives. Yes, he hadn't hit me, but he had used sexual violence towards me and been very aggressive, like that very day. How many times had he forced himself on me? How many times had he raped me? Although he wouldn't call it rape. He called it 'his right'.

And, what about the time just before we came to the UK that he was going to strangle me with the griddle? All this was not acceptable for anyone. It was abuse, whether sexual, mental, physical or emotional. For our three-year-old to witness this was unforgivable.

I kept asking him why he said that it was OK for men to hit their wives; why did he say that men are their wives' keepers and so women should have the decency to shut up when the husband is angry, and then she wouldn't have to be hit. He justified all this by saying that no man would hit his woman over nothing, so it would be her fault. I asked him if this was the case for us as well, to which he replied, 'Of course.' He said his mother used to remain silent when his father was angry, and I was too spoilt, otherwise I would have known all this anyway. So in other words, it is the fault of the person who has made the other person angry and not the fault of the one who cannot control or manage their anger!

We were both shouting. He was swearing at me too, which made Haari very much afraid. He didn't need to witness this. He was crying, standing next to me, holding and hugging my legs tightly. Suhaan would not let me pick him up. It was as if he was ignorant of the fact that Haari, our child together, was watching. I started crying because Haari was crying, his eyes and nose were running. Suhaan then became even more angry, shouting and asking why I was crying for nothing.

'Is this nothing?' I asked.

'Women are only good for one thing,' he replied and then started to pull off my sari.

I stood there, not holding my son or with my hands on his head, but covering my bust. He ripped off my red blouse and unbuckled my bra strap. Still holding my hair for control, he threw the bra off my body. I stood still, disgusted at what my son could see. He looked up as my silent tears ran from my eyes onto his head. His tears ran onto his shirt as he sobbed away loudly.

I begged for forgiveness but he took no notice. I pleaded but to no avail, and then I told the truth. He didn't like the fact that I had hated all his dominance and I didn't want to take him back, but for Haari's sake I did.

He replied in a mocking manner, 'Well at least I've got my son to thank for his mother doing me such a big favour. But now let me tell you something for nothing. I only married you because you were British, and so that's why I've been on my best behaviour.'

I laughed back saying, 'You have that nationality already!'

'Well I have the nationality but not the passport, and my friends say that until then I must behave, otherwise you may tell immigration, and then I won't get it.'

'Now you won't get it,' I spat back at him.

With that, he gagged my mouth with my sari and started to grope and touch all my private areas like a disgusting animal. My mouth was tied so tightly I had to breathe through my nose, but my hair was free. Because of all his pulling and tugging at my hair I would often have bad headaches the following day. His arm swept around my neck to keep me in one place. He did his manly thing, and after a few minutes of that, he had finished. He left me to cry, sob and cope with it anyhow I liked, but how did my son cope with it, I thought. That was my main worry. I was twenty years of age, and so naïve.

We had had this performance before and I had learnt why it hadn't been repeated for a while, but why had it happened again now? What kind of mother was I? What kind of woman was I? What kind of human was I? Would I like to have witnessed these scenes as a child? Would they have left me traumatised? Was I a good human being? Was I a good role model for my child, or indeed this society? I knew it really was the time for *a final farewell to my love*, my only love, never to be replaced.

A Night of Compassion, Mind and Body

'HAPPY BIRTHDAY, SON.'

'Thank you, Mama.'

'You are getting so tall, Haari. You are nearly as tall as me.'

He stood smiling at me as I kissed his forehead. His warm, grey-brown eyes shone directly at me like the sun outside shining on its land. His smile as wide as his father's, but somehow his personality had not been tainted by him at all. Haari remained soft, gentle and kind yet assertive. There was no ruthlessness in his behaviour or attitude at all. He was the spitting image of his father, except for his colour, which was very light, like mine. He was tall, medium built, and even though he did not really have much influence from his father, as strange as it may be, he always wore his hair long like him, shook his head like him, smiled like him and had the same table manners, hurrying his food as if someone is standing with a shotgun to his head.

'Can I go and play outside for a while?'

'Yes, of course. Are you excited about going out tonight?'

'Yes, Mama, especially as my friends will be there.'

I smiled back at him and, as always, I placed both of my hands over on his head to create a perfect parting in his hair, just the way I liked it, on him and myself, after all that's what my mother used to do to me, keeping my hair sleek and straight, as it still is today. Haari, as always, smiled back and put his fingers right through his hair so it stood up, just the way he liked it, just like his father's – funky and spiky, and yes, cool!

His favourite clothes, like mine, were joggers, T-shirts and trainers, just like I used to wear, but had not for a long time. I looked on at him while he played football with the boys outside, exactly where I used to play. His friends were relatives of some of my old friends. How strange what life throws at us.

That evening Haari and I went to a local pizza restaurant where his friends joined us. I left the boys there to eat, drink and enjoy their food, while I joined Charlie in a separate corner to eat. We could hear them talking and laughing, joking about girls, football and school. I was at peace listening to him having fun. They had all eaten and then the staff brought the birthday cake. They lit the eleven candles on the cake. Haari looked on with excitement, not because of the cake, but because of his friends. The cake was a must on all of his birthdays and all of my twenty-eight birthdays, except maybe for one in India.

The boys all ate the cake, while we took photographs of all of them. It was a good evening. We came back home and sat with our milky hot chocolate. I asked him why he did not wear smarter clothes. He laughed and replied that joggers and T-shirts were much more comfortable.

'Honestly, why can't you wear smart clothes sometimes, at least on your birthday you should have. We bought both sets for you – smart and sporty. Just to keep me happy you should have.'

He looked at me, the glint in his eyes warmed with the cheeky smile on his face, pondering on what I had just said. Suddenly he said, 'That is exactly what your mama used to say, isn't it?'

'Yes it is; my mama and your nanno.'

'Nanno?'

'Nanno or grandmother, same thing, but then you've never used these words, so how would you know?'

'From the things that you have told me, Mama, you are just like your mama.'

'Well I never used to be. I used to be like my papa.'

'Am I like my papa or you?' he asked.

'Well you should know, Haari. You see him every weekend. But I'd say that you look like him, and your personality is like mine,' I ventured.

With these words we both started laughing and the only thing that kept going round in my mind was that, if I had turned into my mama, then just imagine Haari turning into his mama or worse still, his papa? For girls to turn out like their mother would seem to be a good thing in our culture and society, but for boys to be caring and gentle, it's almost not the done thing; our culture and religion teaches boys to be macho, big, hard, strong and to be decision makers, leaders. Daughters are meant to be obedient girls who follow the leader, whom they obey without question. They bow to their religion and culture without thinking and questioning their role in society or as an individual.

My son, Haari, my big boy, a lot like me but when in a crowd of people I would be able to recognise him as being Suhaan's son. Haari had been through quite a lot while his father was living with us but, since we parted, things had become very much settled. Over the years I have been his inspiration and his role model. We have kept each other company and, truthfully speaking, it has not been an uphill struggle or a downhill turmoil. A few years have gone by since the last storm at home, but then that was much too great to put up with any longer. Thinking back, I really would have put up with all the rest from Suhaan, but that last scene, in front of a child, his own child – he was blind to everything but his own sexual fantasies, blind to everyone else's feelings.

I still think back on it and think deeply as to the question of what was the greatest sin. If I had put his sexual habits or sexual abuse to one side of the scale, and all the rest of his deeds, good as well as, or course, bad, how would the scale have tilted? What side would have outweighed the other? Sexual abuse was not a term used much in those days, and it may seem really strange, but to a Westerner it is a sin, it is illegal. But for someone who comes from my mother's part of the world it was acceptable: a man had the right to do that. It was a normal part of being hungry for your wife. It was natural and all the women who have come from my mother's village say it is not a sin. It was maybe not the nicest of things but definitely not a sin; more just lust of a man wanting a woman so badly. For the newer generation, well, their feelings are totally different. They no longer think that it is acceptable for a woman to be forced into anything and taken advantage of because she is physically weaker than the male – no really does mean no.

I really did hope and pray, as a Hindu and a Christian, that these scenes had not left my Haari scarred for life. He seemed to have coped with those memories pretty well considering the fact that he does remember bits. Sometimes I think he told me that he only remembers the not so bad bits just to make me feel better, and other times he selected what he would like to remember and tell me. Maybe that was also a way that he coped with it himself. Whatever the thought, he coped with it remarkably well.

I think that Haari was right in saying that I had turned into my mother. I say that with regret because I know that I think more like her than my papa. He would have said walk out of the marriage straight away, but she would not. She always said that it is the woman who makes all the sacrifice for the marriage and puts children first ahead of her own marital bliss or happiness. It is undeniable that I also thought like that, since I had got married and had the twins, or maybe even before when life was all about Mama and the sacrifices I made for her. Or was I just a foolish child? I really can't say. I do know one thing for sure – I would have let him back into our lives, given our distorted marriage another go, for Haari's sake, not mine.

That shameful night ended when I finally put Haari to bed and dozed off in the process myself. I awoke at midnight and the wetness between my legs meant that I was too uncomfortable to doze off to sleep again. I got up to clean myself and so headed off to the bathroom. I could hear the television still on and I slowly went down to the bend in the stair, leaving Haari cuddled up with Cookie in bed. I could hear him chuckling away to someone on the phone, telling him about his passionate, sensual and erotic love-making. He described it as if someone had gone to heaven and back; in other words experiencing something that you only dream about but never live. He kept saying disgusting things like what you might see in a blue movie or pornographic video: the thinness of her waist, the long, black, bewitching magic of her hair, the tightness of her sari clasping her white body, the draping of the thin cloth of the sari around her, the blouse hugging her sensual, gigantic assets...

Apart from this side of him, everything else I could have put up with. Why couldn't he learn? Why couldn't he behave himself? It was almost as if he was sharing me with his friends. How would they look at me and how would I look at them? I slowly went back upstairs. After about ten minutes there was a knock at the door. He was surprised and just stared at the front door. He saw me come down and said quickly, 'I wonder who it could be at this time of night. Forget them, don't open it!'

'All things evil come out at night. We're still awake and so are they,' I said.

With that I opened the door. Those were our final words to each other. The police escorted him away once he had hurriedly gathered some of his things, not that he had much. He never bought anything for himself. It was always me who did that, with my money, not his. He always send his money to his parents back home. He showed no regret or remorse as he looked at me from the front step for the last time. As he did so he held out his right hand as if to shake mine. I owed him that much, so I shook his hand and nodded politely. I then saw his British passport on a pile of letters. I took it and gave it to him for I knew that he would have had to come back for it. I didn't tell the police the full details and I didn't press any charges. I just wanted some peace and harmony in my life with my son, and that was what I had from that point onwards.

Suhaan and I didn't speak when we met. He talked to Haari and Haari, in return, talked to him happily. They communicated well and I never stopped him from seeing his son at the weekends. Our marriage did not exist any more but we were not divorced: we were separated and free agents. I did not know what was on his mind, but as for me, I would remain single and always remembered as Haari's mama and Suhaan's wife, or who knows, his ex-wife, but that would not be my choice and so far has not been his choice either. All his messages for me were passed through Haari and vice versa. Usually they were about Haari.

Why is it that men have to do things like that? But then, there are also women who behave like this too? Nonetheless, why did Suhaan have to do all that? If he hadn't we may have still been together. I never wanted to marry him but then I never wanted to be separated from him either. My marriage, even though through force, was not meant to end. No, that's the wrong word, as it hasn't ended yet. We were not meant to be separated. Our son was not meant to grow up with parents who had separate lives. That was the worst thing about all of this mess. Haari was the one who suffered, not that it showed. No child in the world should have to grow up with one parent and the other only part-time. A child, every child, needs the stability and normality of life with both parents together.

I cannot change that now, but do hope that he always remains very close to his father. They do love each other and I'm sure they are buddies. I say buddies because both Suhaan and I were young parents, and so, as you can imagine, Suhaan was very much a young man still and had not matured like some. Maybe this was because he was always a mummy's boy and never had a chance to really grow up.

Growing up was not one of Suhaan's strong points, for even now he still lives with a male friend of his and works on and off with no real commitment. He still sends money home to his parents, doesn't cook or clean as the mother of the friend does all that, and because they are Indians, they feel that it is the woman's role to cook and clean. One more to care for makes no difference. Obviously they also feel sorry for him as well because his wife had him thrown out of his home, they would say. She was a terrible young rebel, but then what else would you expect from a little hussy like her. She was half white and whites do not have strict beliefs any more. Having said that neither did her trollop of a mother for she had a good upbringing but eloped shamefully with a white man, bringing shame to the family name and tarnishing the Asian culture. Oh well, one cannot control what other people say; everyone has a right to an opinion.

Since Suhaan was no longer living with us and Haari was getting older, we decided that, once he was eleven years of age, we should no longer stay in the room together, and for privacy's sake perhaps he should have his own room. He wanted to keep the one he had already made his. I moved my things into my parent's room, even though it was still a tearful move: firstly because I was leaving Haari, even though he was in my room and with my companion Cookie whom he no longer hugged, and secondly because I could remember my papa in the master bedroom. I sometimes wondered if Haari had told anyone that he still shared a bed with his mother. Would it have been acceptable in society, as nowadays it certainly is not? But then again, we are Asians and such things are acceptable.

I hung some of my clothes in my papa's wardrobe and put the rest in my mama's cupboard. This way I shared a space with them both. Papa's clothes were still hanging in the wardrobe as if he was going to need them soon. His shoes were still sparkling clean, smelling of boot polish, as if it was yesterday, and yet it was years and years since they'd been worn. His expensive aftershaves were still paraded on the dressing table, along with Mama's things. His cufflinks, with inscriptions on them, were still there, as was his pillow where he used to sleep, just the way he liked it, close to Mama's, slightly touching, giving them both space and yet having togetherness as well.

I dared not sleep on their bed so I slept on the cabin bed, where Suhaan had slept for quite a while. I had slept so often on this bed and yet this time I felt so bad – me there but my parents absent. That first night was full of reflections and thoughts, and a heart that ached all night long. It really did haunt me all night – the absence of them three, one, through no choice of his own, and the other, through her own choice. And Suhaan, the bed he made himself, laid in himself, and then left the bed – for me. That night was one of many when I lay awake, but I did not want to disturb Haari with my own insecurities. Slowly but surely I became accustomed to sleeping in that room, on my own, in my old bed.

As Haari had been in school since the age of four, it meant I had time on my hands to explore new ventures for myself. I started working part-time, which meant that I had just a little more money but a lot less time. It was good as it meant that I was finally getting some prospects back into my life, which I was being paid for. I worked as a sales assistant and met many people daily. This job had definitely meant that I was missing my parents a lot less, and more to the point, missing Suhaan a lot less too. When Haari started his secondary school I knew I would be extending my hours at work a bit more, but not so much that I was not at home for him when he got in from school. I was no longer dropping him off or picking him up as he said that he was too big now.

Even so, I did not want to be out when he was home and so that was how our life was. Whenever Haari was home I was sure to be there. I really did not want to miss out on any of his growing up, the way it had been for me until that fateful day which seemed a long, long time ago. Everything was perfect before then, before the death of my papa, my dearest papa, Thomas Craven, Doctor Thomas Craven. I used to say that name with such pride and had wanted to step into his shoes myself and become a doctor. I am useless as I am not a doctor or a patient. Now my family lives in his house, without my parents. Was I really to blame for his death? Was I really the 'killer child'?

The deadly reunion I had had with my father was in the morgue when I could see the colour of love erased from his face because he could not see his one and only child any more. In comparison to other reunions I have had, not that there have been many, this was the most daunting and upsetting one of all even though I still get upset when I visit the graveyard. This reunion was not, indeed, of anyone's own choice, but more of an acceptance of my own life. This life had been almost like a chapped lip but without any soothing balm: the discomfort, the unpleasantness with no choice.

My own childhood years was a time that academically I was best at, a time when I should have been building all my bricks together to form a good, rock-solid foundation for myself and for my future, but I was taken out of school to a land far away, full of fresh memories and an uncertain future. That was not my doing but the choice of someone who was so close and so dear. This was her fault, not mine, but I had to suffer the consequences. Our 'holiday' which had lasted a lifetime, with a new disillusioned beginning, her marriage, was her choice. My marriage was due to my desperation for freedom, my error of innocence. The cruelty from one person to another makes me question the humane judgement behind a male's dominance, control and superiority over women, and yet women do that also. My mother did it to me! She caused me my tears, tears of betrayal and yes, I did shed many 'tears of silence'.

I had no freedom, no choice, just had to accept the circumstances and decisions made for me. Why? It was because I was a child, a child bride who had shed a lot of tears. Tears and betrayal and more tears because the one person who had bonded his own flesh and soul with mine turned out to only accept what was good in me so long as I was good. So long as I performed and bewitched him with my hair, 'the darkness of the night', then all would be well. But surely he was supposed to have been mine for ever; he was the one I shed all those tears behind the veil for. Where had the love and respect gone? Like they say, underneath the feet of a mother, which I was, lies heaven, so therefore a male must respect the female for she gives the male life. His first breaths as he is born into this world after being cradled in the womb for nine months, are due to the woman risking her own life to give life to another – a mother's sacrifice, her own blood, sweat and tears. How remarkable is that! But does a woman even have the same status as a man?

If I had been a boy, if Sani had been a boy, would he have been taken abroad? I do not think so. In the circumstances of being sexually, verbally and physically abused, he would not have been. He would have been a first-class citizen, not a second-class citizen as I was, as Sania was, and in the eyes of some, especially men, will remain so for ever. A woman who throws out her husband means that she has taken steps to thinking and making decisions for herself and not made by the man, so in the eyes of men, and still in small-minded people, including women, she has become too free, not thinking right and too independent. You are, as a female, allowed to make decisions so long as the strings are pulled by a man; we had to keep toeing the line.

It's strange that when a man has an extra-marital affair society says that he has just made a mistake and men like to sow their oats in various places. Maybe just a quick romp in the hay, plenty of love but maybe no regret. But a woman, in the same circumstances, is given a particular name – a whore, a slut, a slapper – but never is it said that she made a mistake. There are different rules for each sex, but why? Are women not allowed to be as independent as men? Are they never going to be allowed to make their own decisions? If women do not dominate men, why does it happen the other way around or do women do that also? Why is it, even today, we are still being forced into marriages but men are not, or definitely not as much? Men are breaking free but society will not allow women to do so. Why is physical abuse still so rife for the silent sufferers and a sin if they report it? Why is it that we, humans, accept verbal abuse? We are asked to ignore the anger of our partner so he can be allowed to calm down, and anyway, men are allowed to get angry.

You would hardly hear that women have sexually abused a man, and if you did, it is wrong, but when a man does it within a marriage, they say it was not rape. If they are married then it is his *right*. What rights do we women have? We have to hold the family together. My mother did not at one point, and I definitely did not. What would people say about us, or women like us? We would have a sale tag on our backs with a low price on it. That would be our reward, and grateful we should be for it.

Even language is created with a male bias. For example, take the word *man-made*: has anyone ever thought of calling something *woman-made*? Of course not, and I know I am not naïve or ignorant, and the word *man* is used in relation to human species as a whole, so why are we not treated equally as a whole? Why couldn't we all have been born equal, everyone the same? Adam and Eve both came into the world as equals, didn't they? So when did this segregation of the sexes actually begin?

Was my life ordinary? Was it full of hope and glory, or was it indeed a life of optimism? Or perhaps a lot of pessimism? Maybe these words do not actually describe what had happened to me. Maybe it is, actually, exactly what happens if you are an Asian or a female. Some may say that I was hoping for the greener side of life and saw the events in my life negatively. Perhaps, just perhaps, it could be that life really holds no guarantees of happiness or of equality. Maybe a woman's life is full of sacrifices like my sacrifice for my mother's freedom. What is freedom? Surely it's your own interpretation of the word. What is love? Is it an under-standing, a joy, trust or a beautiful feeling of intimacy between two people? Whatever it is I didn't receive it from Suhaan even though I was probably craving it. I know that I would have sacrificed my own happiness just to keep him with us. I would have done anything to keep my double miracle alive, my son Kez, so that I could have forever smelt my beloved's sweet breath.

Is this the way that a girl's life – whether as mother, daughter, sister or wife – is supposed to be and are decisions really supposed to be made for you, without your permission? Maybe a child is meant to be a child, and not have to face tears and desolation. Maybe events like those that happened to me just make children grow up quickly and face responsibility at a young age. It's not just women's lives that get turned upside down, but also men's as well. It's not just men who force women or show aggression towards them but women do also. Is all of this normal – just the good with the bad? Was my life good and bad? Has this story revealed painful secrets and has Sania's dreams deserted her?

The years went by. Suhaan had found work in a local factory and was renting a room. He had progressed. When we did meet, we never spoke, merely glanced at one another. He kept coming at the weekends to collect his son and always brought him back safely. If Haari did not want to go he would tell him. It all seemed fine. It was a happy enough arrangement, but a shame we weren't together. I think if he had apologised, or tried to make amends, I may have forgiven him. He made no attempts at reconciliation, and nor did I. He remained single, and so did I. There seems to be no more 'dire consequences' but at least the final farewell to my love was peaceful.

Haari had done well in school and followed in his grandfather's footsteps by gaining entry into medical college. He was happy. I was also happy as, while he was in secondary school, I got my qualifications and also applied to study medicine. Naturally I was not going to study at the same place as him. He was a young medical student and I, a mature student. We were mother and son, born of different circumstances – too different to be in the same working and studying environment.

These last few years I was quite content to have lived a pleasant and comfortable life, but also a busy one. There were less thoughts and reflections as now Haari and I were both well-adjusted to one another. I had forgotten the past, or rather, put it behind me where it really belonged, and was at the stage where everything seemed good once again, except for one thing: my lost childhood. Apart from that it was all good. The years when Haari was in the infant and junior schools afforded me time for a lot of adjustment – getting over the past and trying to move on. I was getting used to never having Mama and Papa ever again, and this was the way we liked it.

Late one summer afternoon, Haari had been out with his friends. They had all driven to Blackpool. He got back pretty late, and after having a little bit to eat, he was ready for bed. For an eighteen-year-old boy he was still, almost, like a child, going to sleep quite early. Before he went off to bed we talked about how excited we were about starting our study of medicine a few months down the line. We talked about how we could compare notes, help each other with work and so on. I told him that, for now, it was better just to enjoy the summer holidays while we could as, come September, we would both be very busy.

In the last few years, while you could say that I found my independence, I had started to wear English clothes as well, even though the aunties down the road and in town gave me strange looks. They spoke bitterly about me, 'She has no shame. Married, kicked out her husband, has a child to set an example to and look at her in those tight English clothes.' But then, who cares? And no, I didn't wear joggers all the time!

When I went to college I always wore English clothes, and at university I would need them again, but at home, I still wore my saris.

As Haari went up to bed around ten o'clock, just before the news, I thought that I may as well have a quick shower before watching the rest of the programme. As I was about to get out of the bathroom I heard Haari rush down to open the door. I wrapped my hair with a towel and listened to who was at the door. He asked the person to come inside and to be seated. I came downstairs and, as I did so, it was as if a gust of wind had spread a scent around the room; a scent that I was well acquainted with. I looked at Haari while ignoring all my senses. His face was pale. I smiled and asked him who it was. He just turned his head towards the person sitting on the sofa. I felt tense and worried. What was that smell that I experienced just a few seconds ago? I took the towel off my head and let my long, black hair drape down my back. I could see the back, or rather only the head of this person. It was almost like mine: the same colour hair, dark black.

I said, quietly, 'Hello.'

I could see that the person on the sofa was definitely female. She got up and with her back still turned to me she replied, ever so softly, 'Hello.'

I could see the long, black, straight hair draped down her back, just like mine, although mine was still wet. She was identical to me.

'Hello,' I said, this time a little louder.

'Hello, Sania,' she said as she turned around.

I stood there lifeless and still, then I looked at Haari. His eyes were damp with tears. He was waiting for my reaction. I looked away from him and looked at her as she said, 'Oh, Sania, you are still the same little girl, still in joggers and T-shirts. Thank goodness that some things have not changed,' she sighed.

I did not feel like talking much because my emotions were all over the place. There were so many questions, but not now. It was too late. Haari asked her if she wanted to eat or drink. She shook her head and then said that she needed to rest as she had made a long journey. Haari looked at her bags and told her that he would take them up to her room. She followed, he led, and I remained still, so very still. Was she just tired or unwell, and why had she come back? Why now? Why now, when I had got used to life without her? I didn't want to talk to her. Was I trying to convince myself? Why... why was I denying myself, and her, what should be natural? Her voice seemed very sorrowful but I was still hurting so badly. All those feelings that I thought I had laid to rest were being rekindled once again.

As I went up she was already fast asleep in her own bed. I looked at her, at peace with herself. She lay where Papa's body used to lay, her arms stretched out as if they were asleep together, her arms under and over him. I slipped into my own bed and for once, after almost a lifetime, I dozed off without a care in the world.

I still hoped that Maansi would write and give me some good news of her own. I don't know if she will or not, but I live in hope – hope that she will reply to my letter, which I have sent her since my arrival back in England. She hadn't replied, but then neither had my mother, and now she was here in her bed, with my letters to her still near the telephone. I had regularly phoned Beeji, Badi Ma, Suhaani Ma and more so Moti Masi.

How and why did this have to happen? Why now? Why not before, why not when I needed her – the one and only person I had in the world – my mama.

I did feel hurt and betrayed by her but then it was also as if my family was not complete, a bit of the old and a bit of the new, my son. Life felt normal for the first time in a very long time. That night as I first caught a glimpse of her eyes, I saw he eyes half open, the same tired look which I saw many years ago when my father died. That time, she was tired and sad. Now she looked tired but there wasn't any sadness in her eyes. In fact, there seemed to be a sigh of relief. I knew that Dev had died and that tiresome night brought her back to her old life again.

Many thanks to my daughter, Thaiba Razzia Mehrban, who inspired me to write about the character of Maya, her mother and sister.

A Child

I came into the world without a choice,
And yet at my birth there was great rejoice.
A child was born and showered with love,
We two sisters enjoyed all the life and above.
This short life and happiness had a tainted smell,
As the leaf from the heaven tree into our garden
    fell.
We saw it coming with the gust of wind and rain,
We knew its message was tainted with pain.
She slept one night, unaware of the world,
We all called out furiously, as we all hurled.
At her and at God to reawaken her mind,
Alas, to deaf ears as God was not being so kind.
He laid her to rest;
We carried on with our best,
Without the love of a woman's breast.
She came another into our broken life,
A mother figure who became our father's wife.
She showered us with memories of a mother we
    didn't have,
A child could see her happiness and her three
    that we did have,
We both rejoiced and laughed, as we played with
    the three,
As we loved them all with a happy, big glee.

They are a big part of the me that I know,
They hold me to my father who showed me life
    that I know.
A child to a father, full of pride and respect,
A life of longing but safe haven I was kept.
He showed me life and the miles I had to walk,
Never be weak and aim for the sky he did talk.
His memory lives on, in all five of us today
As we still live, as they both lay
In the mud that cradled my mother one day.
A child reflects on the life she has made,
Tears of silence she has shed but hopefully won't
    fade.
Tears behind the veil of which, she will live to
    adorn,
As she learns the reality, of life and the dead she
    still mourns.